MW01275419

Immaculate Misconception

By

Joel Bartow

Jeff,

Since you like my stories so much, try this one.

Regards,

J Bartow
2003

© 2002 by Joel Bartow. All rights reserved.

No part of this book may be reproduced, stored in a retrieval system, or transmitted by any means, electronic, mechanical, photocopying, recording, or otherwise, without written permission from the author.

ISBN: 1-4033-5778-1 (e-book)
ISBN: 1-4033-5779-X (Paperback)
ISBN: 1-4033-5780-3 (Dustjacket)

Library of Congress Control Number: 2002093535

This book is printed on acid free paper.

Printed in the United States of America
Bloomington, IN

1stBooks - rev. 11/1/02

CHAPTER ONE

"That's not what I'm saying, Michael. I'm saying that you have to take it all or nothing. You can't pick and choose the parts you like and ignore the rest of it."

"I'm not ignoring anything," Michael said calmly. "I am saying that the Gospels were not written independently of each other but were instead built on each other. With each successive Gospel, we hear an updated argument against the continuing philosophical attacks on the new Christianity."

The other seminary student was not as well read as Michael, which was one of the reasons he was having trouble understanding the point Michael was trying to make.

"What do you mean? What philosophical attacks?" David Owens, who had a private room at the end of the hall, wondered how Michael Dennis would ever become a priest with these wild opinions about the Bible.

"Professor Mink, of Lincoln University in Missouri, calls it story-mongering, where story and claim beget antistory and counterclaim."

"I don't understand. What counterclaims?" David asked. Michael was beginning to understand why this seminarian had failed his senior seminar once already. Owens wasn't the brightest candle in the tabernacle, which didn't make him very popular. Looking into David

Owens' pale, thin face, Michael regrouped his thoughts and continued.

"David, almost all Bible scholars agree that the Gospel of Mark is the oldest of the four Gospels, and John is the latest. In Mark, we get a simple telling about Jesus. Matthew added some things to answer the skeptics that reacted to Mark. Then Luke answered critics of Matthew, and John added even more stuff after that."

"For instance?"

"In Mark, Jesus is called a carpenter. There must have been some backlash about a lowly carpenter being the Messiah, because Matthew changed it to the carpenter's son. Luke must have been thinking about the public perception of carpenters when he left out any such references at all."

"Are you really going to turn in a term paper questioning the motives of Matthew, Luke and John?"

"Each of the Gospels is told from a different point of view. Each point of view has a different motive. Mark was written for Jews living outside Israel, while Matthew was written for Jews inside Israel, and Luke was written to appeal to Gentiles. Why can't I say that?"

"Why not? Shit, Michael, for one thing Father Quinn will have a fit, and he'll probably give you an F!" David rubbed the dark circles under his sunken eyes.

"I'm not worried about old Father Quinn," Michael said as he left David Owens' room and walked down the hall of the dormitory to his own.

"You should be!" David yelled after him. "I'm not taking his seminar for the second time because I liked it so much the first time."

Father Quinn had a reputation of being a difficult teacher and was in his fourth year of teaching at the Seminary of the Immaculate Conception, a university level seminary on New York's Long Island, which looked more like an Austrian castle than a school. The seminarians just called the place "I.C." A twenty-five-year veteran priest, Father Quinn taught the senior-level theology seminar, in which every senior had to present a reasonably original theological idea and defend it in front of the whole class. While the assignment was to present an original idea, Father Quinn was already known for his dislike of revisionist history where the New Testament was concerned. Quinn would prefer to have homosexuals ordained as priests than freethinking troublemakers. Father Quinn already had his eye on Michael Dennis, who he considered too intelligent for his own good.

A good-looking young man with brown hair and green eyes, Michael Dennis was the son of an unwed immigrant mother. His mother, Nellie, had come to America from Russia at age ten with her Polish Catholic mother after her Russian Communist father, Anatoly Denisov, died. Nellie's mother came to live with Nellie's uncle in New York. Due to anti-Russian sentiment during the cold war, they changed their last name to Dennis. At age ten, Ninel Denisov became Nellie Dennis. At age sixteen, Nellie became pregnant. Being a strict Catholic, abortion was out of the question, so her mother moved the family to St. Louis, Missouri to have the baby and start anew. When

Nellie had Michael, he became the pride and joy of both his mother and grandmother, and the old life in Brooklyn was forgotten.

The heavy Catholic influence from his grandmother led Michael Dennis to attend St. Thomas Aquinas High School Seminary in Hannibal, Missouri. From there he went on to college at Immaculate Conception in New York. Although Nellie Dennis worked hard cleaning houses, they could not afford to send Michael to the seminary. Michael's great uncle, the brother of his grandmother, had done well for himself in the clothing business in Brooklyn and had paid for all of Michael's expenses. Uncle Joseph had always said it was worth it to have a priest in the family.

Uncle Joseph went to church regularly at St. Peter and Paul Catholic Church in the Bay Ridge area of Brooklyn, but he was also a regular at the Czarina Restaurant in Brighton Beach, which was run by a former Ukrainian boxer turned enforcer for the Russian mob. The FBI had noticed that Joseph Komkovsky visited the Czarina almost every Monday, the one day of the week that the restaurant was closed. The banquet room in the back of the Czarina was used as a meeting place for some unsavory, muscle-bound characters in black leather coats. The FBI speculated that perhaps there was a link between Joseph's trips to the Czarina and the two warehouse fires that had netted him hefty insurance payments during economic hard times. But then, the FBI was cynical about things like that. Joseph Komkovsky swore to all his friends that the fires were completely accidental, but some of Joseph's friends were just as cynical as the feds.

* * * * *

As the day of Michael's thesis presentation approached, the anticipation grew. Many of the seminarians had become sounding boards for Michael's theory about the Gospels as an evolution of pro-Christian propaganda. Most of those who knew the topic of Michael's thesis expected a firestorm when he presented it. It would be a class they did not want to miss.

Each night, one of the seminarians would be unable to resist asking Michael a question about his "theory of evolution of the Gospels." Tonight it was his roommate, Greg, a fat, ugly, nearsighted youth that everyone liked. Greg looked at Michael over glasses with smudged lenses and fired off his question.

"What is an example of something that is significantly different in the four Gospels and your proposed explanations for those differences?"

"Just look at the beginning of the first three Gospels," Michael said, his green eyes showing his enthusiasm for the subject. "It is as plain as the nose on your face. In Mark's Gospel, the first mention of Jesus is at his baptism by John the Baptist. There was no prediction of his birth, no angels, no slaughter of innocent babies, or anything like that. In the Old Testament, prophets or angels or voices from the sky, foretold the births of important characters. The people who read Mark in the first century must have wondered why Jesus' birth was not such a grand event. So, in Matthew, we get a birth story. Matthew starts out by making sure of the bloodline back to King David, fourteen generations from Abraham to David and twenty-eight generations from David to Jesus. Matthew doesn't address the problem that the line of King David goes through Joseph, who is not really the biological father of Jesus, but I digress. Matthew has an angel appear to Joseph, telling him not to be afraid to take Mary, who is with child even though she and Joseph have not been together, as his wife. In other words, the angel tells Joseph that Mary hasn't been sleeping around. The angel tells Joseph that it is God's son & they are to name him Jesus. This story caused claims by non-Christians that Jesus was a bastard, or *mamzer*, maybe even fathered by a Roman soldier, which was a real insult back then. So, Luke comes along and changes the story. Instead of appearing to Joseph, the angel appears to Mary, telling her that she will conceive the Son of God through the Holy Spirit. Luke doesn't even tell us how Mary told Joseph. That is a pretty big difference, but it was made to stop the idea furthered by Matthew that Jesus was a *mamzer*."

"You have got to be bleeping kidding me, Michael! You aren't really going to tell Quinn that Matthew screwed up his Gospel, so people started to think Jesus was a bastard, and Luke had to fix it, are you?"

"I think the differences between Matthew and Luke are clearly there. Why do you think the Catholic Church has adopted the version of the annunciation from Luke instead of Matthew? Heck, the Annunciation to Mary is even a holy day now. There has to be a logical reason for it, Greg."

"Oh, man! You have some set of stones."

"There's more to it than just the annunciation," Michael continued. "Matthew made up a whole story about three wise men following a star, Jesus being born in Bethlehem, as predicted by the prophets, and King Herod wanting to kill the future king of the Jews. Matthew has Herod kill all the male babies of the Jews, just like the Pharaoh did in Egypt when Moses was born. Matthew also neglects to mention what Joseph and Mary were doing in Bethlehem or why Jesus was born there. People who knew that Joseph and Mary lived in Nazareth must have questioned Jesus' birth in Bethlehem, so along comes Luke to the rescue again. Luke explains the Bethlehem problem with a census, where Joseph has to go back to his hometown of Bethlehem to be counted in a census conducted by the governor of Syria, Quirinius."

"So, that explains why they were in Bethlehem. Matthew just didn't mention it," Greg offered.

"It isn't that easy. Quirinius did have a census, but he became governor of Syria ten years after King Herod the Great died. King Herod died in 4 BC, so he couldn't have been there to talk to the wise men or kill any babies. Luke was just answering a criticism that questioned the Bethlehem birth. He just…"

"Screwed up?"

"You might say that," Michael smiled as he said it.

"No," Greg answered shaking his head of curly dark hair and pushing his glasses further up on his nose, "you might say that. I would never say that, especially to Father Quinn."

“For Pete’s sake, Quinn is a priest, not the flipping boogieman!”

“Wanna bet?” Greg asked trying to act serious. “Heck, Michael you’re almost a heretic.”

“Did you know that the word heretic means someone who thinks what they want to think instead of what they are supposed to think?”

“In Quinn’s book that makes you a heretic. Four hundred years ago they would have burned you at the stake.”

“Greg, faith is not fairy dust that you can sprinkle on ideas to make them true. The Gospels should not be regarded as historical documents. They are stories that give insights toward Jesus’ overall message of God’s love and that we should love others.”

“The Catholic Church is not going to pay your room and board for the rest of your life to be a philosopher. They are going to expect you to tow the party line and teach that the Gospels are the word of God, not a series of propaganda to rebut early critics.”

“Father Quinn might believe that, but there are other priests who don’t completely subscribe to the party line as you call it.”

“Yeah, maybe, but they’re already priests. You are still in the seminary.”

CHAPTER TWO

On Monday morning, Grant Sherman unlocked the door of his office on the second floor of a hundred-year-old brick house that had been turned into offices. In Princeton, New Jersey, real estate was expensive, so even this modest little walk-up took up a large chunk of the income from his private investigation business. Grant was forty-three and in fairly good shape despite his graying and thinning hair. He was a former Special Agent of the FBI, having served for ten years before walking away from the Bureau's New York Division. Shortsighted supervisors, co-workers ready to tell on you for anything, wide spread incompetence and apathy, and New York City itself had driven him to quit. The supervisors would have said that Grant Sherman had an attitude problem and maybe even a personality problem. Three doctors had given Grant three different diagnoses. He suffered from depression, had bi-polar disorder, or suffered from post-traumatic stress disorder. Grant figured it was probably one of the three. He had been on Paxil, Ativan, Celexa, lithium, and three other mood-altering drugs, but he was still regarded by those who disliked him as an asshole, while those who liked him thought him an excellent investigator and a good guy.

Grant's father had been an angry alcoholic, probably also suffering from some form of depression. When Grant was in college, his father shot Grant's mother in the head with a .357 magnum revolver before turning the gun on himself. That, however, was not the source of Grant's alleged post-traumatic stress. It was growing up in the pressure cooker that he had thought was a normal home until he left it to go to college. Not realizing until he was twenty-years old that he had been an abused child, Grant had always thought that his dad was just an asshole when he got drunk.

Grant didn't let his little family tragedy stop him from finishing college and then a master's degree. He had always dreamed of being an FBI or CIA agent. In fact it was his favorite game as a kid. While other kids played army or baseball, Grant had played "spy."

Three years after leaving the Bureau, Grant had built Sherman Associates into a fairly well known, investigations company. He worked mostly on referrals from satisfied clients and networking at professional seminars, where he taught about fraud and interviewing techniques. He had worked cases on every continent except Australia and Antarctica.

The telephone interrupted Grant's tea making, but he was able to run into the next room and catch it after four rings.

"Sherman Associates, this is Grant," he answered.

"Just the man I wanted to talk to," the voice on the phone said as if Grant should know who it was."

"Yeah," Grant said trying to place the voice.

"I read your update in the alumni newsletter," the voice said.

"Mark!" He placed the voice of his long ago best friend from Notre Dame High School in Easton, Pennsylvania.

"How you doing, buddy? Long time."

"Yeah, it has been a long time."

"I see you left the FBI."

"Yeah, too much Federal and Bureau, but not enough Investigation to suit me."

"I can imagine," Mark O'Shay said.

"What are you up to now?" Grant asked.

"I work for the Archdiocese of New York."

"No shit! How did you pull that off?" Grant asked. He never would have expected the Mark O'Shay he knew to work for the Archdiocese of New York. Mark had jokingly been voted "most likely to be arrested" by his high school classmates.

"Well, you know I was teaching and coaching."

"Yeah."

"Then I got on back at Notre Dame to teach and coach basketball."

"Right, I remember that."

"Well, I had been going to night school at Lafayette College to get my master of education degree."

"And you finally finished it?"

"I finally finished it, man!"

"Congratulations, Mark."

"Thanks. That was last year. One of the guys on the school board at Notre Dame had some connections at the archdiocese here in New York. They had an opening, and here I am."

"So, to what do I owe this phone call?"

"Well, buddy, like I said, I saw you had your own company in the alumni newsletter."

"Uh-huh."

"Well, the Archdiocese of New York needs your professional skills."

"You're kidding! What, someone stealing from the collection plate?" Grant smiled at his own joke.

"No, there was a strange attack on one of our priests."

"An attack? You mean an assault? Did you call the cops?"

"I guess you could call it an assault. No, we didn't get the police involved. You know how the church hates bad press."

"Tell me what happened."

"It happened at the Seminary of the Immaculate Conception in Huntington out on the island. Monsignor Franklin called me the other day to ask me to find a Catholic investigator to look into this quietly for us."

"Look into what? What happened, Mark?"

"Well, it appears that someone was hiding & waiting for one of our priests to leave the school and go to the residence. The person or persons knocked him on the head and took something."

"A mugging? You want me to investigate a mugging?"

"Grant, they took some of the priest's blood."

CHAPTER THREE

"Took some of his blood? How much blood? Is he still alive?"

"Yeah, he seems to be okay. From the purple marks on his arm, I would guess they drew a test tube or two. It didn't take them long – the priest was only out for a minute of two."

"Well, Mark, you're in luck. I just finished a big case in Africa and I have some time to accept your case."

"Great, can you come out to the Seminary in Huntington?"

"Sure, that's about a two-hour drive, give or take, depending on traffic. When do you want to meet?"

"In two hours, give or take."

"Do we know how much the archdiocese is willing to front for this operation?"

"Seventy-five dollars an hour, plus expenses, one hundred dollars an hour for any hours over forty in one calendar week. The calendar week starts on Monday for our purposes."

"Okay, I can live with those terms," Grant said. *And maybe be able to pay the rent on time this month.*

"Fine, I will meet you at the reception area of the seminary with Monsignor Franklin and the priest at eleven o'clock."

"I'll be there. Thanks, Mark."

"No problem, see you at eleven."

Grant hung up the phone and raised his hands over his head in victory. It had been a while between cases.

* * * * *

Immaculate Conception was a large, brick structure with white marble corner stones fitted all the way up to the roof, which was red ceramic tile. In the center of the building a square structure gradually became a flat-topped rotunda as the four corners were blended into ornamentations. The gothic archways around the doorways were all marble with intricate carvings. It was quite a place.

Grant Sherman stood on the sidewalk looking up at the rotunda. *I think they could have afforded more than seventy-five an hour.* Following the walk to what appeared to be the main office, Grant was about to ask a passing student for directions, until he saw a small white sign that read, "Office." He entered and waited for his eyes to adjust from the bright May sunlight to the dark interior of the seminary. Grant, noticing an elderly lady sitting at a desk in the next room, asked for Mark O'Shay and Monsignor Franklin.

"Oh, you must be the gentleman they are waiting for. I'll just tell them you're here." The woman tottered off down the hall.

Mark O'Shay got to the reception area before the elderly messenger.

"Grant, how are you. I guess you didn't have any trouble finding it."

"No," Grant lied, "no trouble at all."

"Monsignor Franklin is waiting to meet you," Mark said walking down the hallway. "He wants you to get started right away."

"I guess I should talk to the priest first."

"Yes, we figured that. The priest is in Monsignor Franklin's office. His name is Father Quinn."

CHAPTER FOUR

Michael Dennis' Great Uncle Joseph was reading the Monday morning edition of *The New York Post*. There was a very interesting AP story that read, "Priests' sexual misconduct costs church." According to the article, The Diocese of Santa Rosa, California had to pay out $16 million to settle a sexual misconduct case against one of their priests. The Diocese of Dallas paid out $30 million. The Archdiocese of Santa Fe, New Mexico almost went bankrupt by paying out over $50 million. The list continued: Tucson, Philadelphia, and then there was Boston, which had even made the cover of *Newsweek.* Some estimates had the Roman Catholic Church paying out about $1 billion to victims of abuse from priests.

"Interesting," Joseph Komkovsky said in a thick accent, turning to the comics. His cell phone on the glass coffee table played a tune from Mozart. "Da," he said into the device, since only Russians knew the number. The voice on the phone spoke carefully, telling Joseph that there was something to discuss. As it was Monday, they agreed to meet at the usual place at two thirty in the afternoon.

* * * * *

As Grant Sherman was led into Monsignor Franklin's office, the shine from the lavishly carved mahogany woodwork was downright distracting. He reached out and ran his hand along the trim of the door.

"Nice isn't it?" Monsignor Franklin asked. "It was carved over seventy-five years ago."

"You have certainly taken good care of it," Grant said.

"My predecessors and I," the gray-haired man in a black cassock said. "I am Monsignor Andrew Franklin," he said extending a hand. Grant grasped the hand and gave it a firm shake.

"Grant Sherman. Nice to meet you."

"Mr. O'Shay tells me that you were an FBI agent in New York City."

"Yes, sir, for ten years."

"Well, I am sure that is qualification enough for our little matter. This is Father Paul Quinn." Monsignor Franklin motioned toward the corner of the room, where a thin, balding man of about fifty years of age sat in a temporarily placed chair. Deferring to Monsignor Franklin, the priest neither stood nor spoke, just nodded to acknowledge Grant's presence.

"Well, I suppose the best thing for me to do would be to interview Father Quinn and figure out where to go from there."

"My thoughts exactly," Monsignor Franklin said. "We have set up everything for you in the conference room at the end of the hall. Mr. O'Shay will show you the way." He extended an arm toward the door. Grant followed Mark O'Shay and Father Quinn to the conference room. It was less ornate than Monsignor Franklin's office, but not much less. Grant chose a chair in the middle of the large oval table, not wanting to be too far away from the interview subject.

"I guess you won't need me in here," Mark said. "I'll be in shouting distance."

"Thank you, Mark," Grant said as Mark closed the conference room door behind him. Grant reached out his hand to Father Quinn. "How are you? Grant Sherman."

"I have been better, Mr. Sherman. This has not been easy, being the object of so much attention from the monsignor."

"I can imagine," Grant said, and he really could. The monsignor had an aura of authority about him like General Patton. "Shall we start at the beginning, Father?"

"There's not that much to tell. I was leaving the chapel at about eight like always."

"You leave the chapel at eight every day?" Grant asked.

"Monday through Friday."

"And this happened when?"

"Friday night."

"Go ahead," Grant urged.

"I was walking along the sidewalk toward the house. As I passed a group of evergreens, I was hit on the head. I didn't lose consciousness right away. I could tell there were two men before I was hit again. I woke up and looked at my watch. Only about five minutes had passed, my sleeve had been rolled up, and there was a small mark on my arm. It eventually got bigger and turned purple." Father Quinn rolled up his sleeve to show Grant a deep purple mark the size of a baseball.

"Ouch!" Grant said. "They must have drawn blood very quickly to bruise you like that. Do you have any idea why someone would take your blood?"

"I am completely at a loss."

"Have you made any enemies?"

"Of course not."

"Have you received any threats?"

"No."

"Have you ever done anything that would upset anyone?" Grant was expecting another negative response, but it didn't come. He waited.

"I have never done anything that would cause someone to attack me like this. Why would they take my blood? I am scared to death! I will have to be tested for HIV exposure! Can you imagine what the press would print about this?"

"Well, Father Quinn, it is a little spooky. The first thing that comes to mind is some Satanist cult needed the blood of a priest for a rite of some kind."

"Oh my word! My blood used in devil worship?" Grant could see how the idea might be very upsetting to a man of the cloth.

"Would you please show me the exact place where the attack happened?"

"Now?"

"Yes, now."

Father Quinn led Grant outside and across the campus toward the chapel. The sidewalk from the chapel was not a straight path, but an appealing ribbon of meandering concrete, which was landscaped on either side with shrubs and flowers. Father Quinn led Grant to a group of three evergreens, which stood about seven feet tall.

"When I passed these three little trees, I was hit from behind. The men must have been waiting behind them," the priest said. Grant was already on his hands and knees looking at the earth inside the triangle of evergreens. There were distinct footprints of two different shoes. Both were flat soled, street shoes, which would be much more difficult to match to prints than boots or tennis shoes would be. There were no cigarette butts, which would have made things easier. He reached into his jacket pocket and removed a roll of yellow twine. Tying one end to one of the evergreens, Grant walked around the three trees several times.

"There," Grant said. "That should keep people from trampling the footprints until I can photograph them and take plaster casts. Can you think of anything else, Father?"

"No, that's all I know."

"Then let's go back to the office."

* * * * *

Uncle Joseph got to the Czarina Restaurant at exactly two thirty. The back door was already unlocked, so he let himself in and walked to the banquet room. The man from the phone was already sitting at the table. Taking a chair across the table, Joseph nodded a greeting.

"So, we have something to talk about?" Joseph asked in Russian.

"Da," the man said and moved his thumb against his two fingers to indicate money.

"You have what I asked for?"

"Da." The man produced a small lunch box.

"Good," Uncle Joseph said, removing a white envelope from his sports coat. After they exchanged items at the same time, the man got up and left. Uncle Joseph took the lunch box and left the Czarina, locking the door behind him.

CHAPTER FIVE

Grant was alone at the conference room table near the monsignor's office with a stack of files, which represented the entire twenty-five-year career of Father Paul Quinn. Grant was thinking about the hesitation the priest had shown after being asked if he had ever done something to upset anyone. Such a hesitation was normal for such a broad, personal question. What bothered Grant was that even after the hesitation, the priest still had not answered the question. Father Quinn had said he had never done anything to make someone want to attack him. So, it was up to Grant to find out what Father Quinn had done to upset someone. *This is not going to be easy.*

Father Quinn's years at the Seminary of the Immaculate Conception had not been smooth ones. There had been complaints from students and parents that Father Quinn was too strict academically. Parents didn't like paying top dollar for seminary school to have some church theology teacher give their sons failing grades in their fourth year. Grant noted the names on the complaint letters.

Prior to I.C., Father Quinn had been assigned to St. Anthony of Padua Catholic Church in the Archdiocese of Boston for sixteen years. There was nothing in his file about any complaints or problems there. "So why the transfer?" Grant asked himself. Reading on, Grant saw that Father Quinn's first priestly assignment had been in Brooklyn over twenty years ago. At that time, he had requested transfer from that parish three times in a six-month period before finally being granted an assignment in Boston. The letters requesting the transfer were in the file. They were short and gave no particular reason for the request other than "personal reasons." The pastor of the parish had not supported the first two requests, but he had supported the third. Apparently the pastor's blessing was all that was required, because Father Quinn was sent packing up to Boston within a month of the third request.

Grant made a note to have Mark O'Shay find him the reason for the transfer of Father Quinn from Boston to I.C. and to remind himself to ask Father Quinn in person why he so adamantly wanted to get out of Brooklyn over twenty years ago. Grant noted the name of the pastor at St. Peter & Paul Catholic Church in Bay Ridge, Brooklyn. He wondered if Father Francis Faye was still around.

* * * * *

The seminar hall was filling up well before the bell, as it was Michael Dennis' day to present his senior theology thesis. Michael was seated at a small table in the front of the room. Father Quinn and another priest would be seated among the students and would pose questions to Michael after his presentation was finished. When the bell rang, silence fell like a brick in the classroom.

"Mr. Dennis, you have the floor," Father Quinn announced from a seat near the back of the room.

"The four Gospels," Michael began in a strong, confident voice, "Matthew, Mark, Luke, & John, are regarded as the basis of our faith in Jesus Christ. Scholars have studied these writings for centuries. One thing almost all experts agree upon is that the Gospel of Mark is the oldest of the four, followed by Matthew and Luke, both of whom used parts of Mark. Matthew and later Luke added things that Mark did not address. What is interesting is that while Matthew and Luke used Mark as a source, they ended up with quite different stories, which are at some points completely contradictory to the others. John, the latest Gospel, is not like the other three, but uses more symbolic language, like Jesus did. However, John too is at odds with the other Gospels about some things. The important thing is not that the Gospels differ or even contradict each other, rather it is why these texts are different that is important."

Father Quinn was already getting angry. He had been aware of the gist of Michael's intended topic and had warned him not to be controversial. It sounded to Father Quinn like a controversy was brewing.

"Perhaps the best place to begin this examination is at the end of the life of Jesus. This is without a doubt the most important event for Christianity, the crucifixion and resurrection of Jesus. So, how could the four Gospels be so different in telling what happened? Are the differences mistakes? I don't think anyone would argue that. I will point out the differences and give logical reasons for these differences. Let's begin with Mark."

"Mark tells us that Pilate, the Roman governor, finds Jesus not guilty of any crimes. However, he gives in to the pressure of the mob and orders Jesus crucified to please them. Pilate's actions are by no means noble. In the later gospels, which were not written just for Jews to read, the actions of Pilate are different. In Matthew, Pilate literally washes his hands of the matter, making the Jewish crowd the executioner of Christ. Luke goes even further, having Pilate appeal to the crowd for Jesus as an innocent man three separate times. However the crowd demands Jesus be put to death. When Romans were being converted to Christianity, the Gospel writers didn't want Romans with Jesus' blood on their hands."

"Next we have the issue of the drinks offered to Jesus while he was on the cross. In Mark, Jesus is offered a drink of wine mixed with myrrh. This would have had an analgesic effect. However, charges surfaced in later years that Jesus had been drugged into a stupor and had not really died on the cross."

"Matthew deals with this problem by making the drink wine mixed with gall, which would have poisoned Jesus, bringing about a quicker, more merciful death. Luke was apparently not satisfied with any drugs being offered. His drink is only sour wine or vinegar, in accordance with the words of Psalm 69:21."

"In another interesting difference between the Gospels, Joseph of Arimathea is described by Mark as a respected and religious man, who is a member of the council, the Sanhedrin. Joseph asks permission to bury the body of Jesus in his own tomb. You can imagine the questions this would raise. Why is a member of the Jewish Sanhedrin, which called for Jesus' execution, offering to bury the body? Matthew picked up on this problem and changed Joseph of Arimathea from a council member to a rich man and disciple of Jesus."

"There is still a problem here: how was it that this rich man was a disciple of Jesus? Jesus taught among the poor and the sick. Luke solves the problem by putting Joseph of Arimathea back into the Sanhedrin, but made him a member who was against the execution of Jesus. So he is taking care of Jesus' body in order to do the right thing."

"One of the most interesting aspects of the evolution of stories in the Gospels is in Matthew. There were always charges that the body of Jesus had been stolen at night by his disciples, who then claimed his resurrection. Matthew places Roman guards at the tomb to refute this idea. John goes even further to eliminate the idea that Jesus was not really dead. John is the only Gospel to mention Jesus being savagely whipped before the crucifixion. John is the only Gospel in which Jesus is nailed to the cross. John specifically mentions that Jesus' legs were not broken. Breaking the legs of a victim of crucifixion was done to speed death. Since the victim would not be able to support his weight with his legs, the pressure on the chest from hanging unsupported would quickly cause suffocation. In John, the guards are coming to break the legs of Jesus, but they find he is already dead. This gives us Roman witnesses to Jesus being dead.

Then, the soldier pierces the side of Jesus with a spear to make sure he is dead. Thus, John ends any speculation that Jesus may have survived the crucifixion."

"If the skeptics could not question whether Jesus was really dead, they could argue that he wasn't really alive again afterward. In Mark, three women go to the tomb to anoint Jesus' body. Now in the first century, women are not considered to be reliable witnesses. The women in Mark's Gospel do not find Jesus, nor do they see any angels. They see a young man who tells them that Jesus has risen. Later, Jesus appears like a vision to the eleven apostles in a room. This is not a very convincing account. Matthew does a better job, having two women going to the tomb and finding an angel. Then the women also see and touch Jesus, who later appears like a vision to the eleven apostles."

"There must have still been some doubt about things, because Luke sent at least five women to the tomb, where they saw two angels. The women tell Peter about it and Peter comes to the tomb to see for himself, giving us a male witness. When Jesus appears to the eleven apostles, he asks for some food and eats fish with them. Ghosts don't eat fish."

"John makes it even better. One woman goes to the tomb and finds it empty. She goes to get Peter and the beloved disciple, two male witnesses. Then two angels appear, and Jesus speaks to the two disciples. Later Jesus appears to the eleven apostles, Thomas is rebuked for doubting that Jesus really arose from the dead, and then Jesus eats fish. How can anyone argue with that?"

"That will be all, Mister Dennis," Father Quinn's voice announced calmly from the back of the room.

"I haven't finished yet, Father."

"Oh, I think you are quite finished. I think we have heard enough of your misconceptions about the inspired writers of the books contained in the Holy Bible, which the Council of Nicaea has determined were authoritative. The church did not make them authoritative, the church leaders in 325 AD sensed that these works were authoritative accounts inspired by God."

"It was at the Council of Nicaea that authority replaced research and faith preempted knowledge," Michael said calmly.

"That is absolutely not the case!" Father Quinn said trying not to lose his temper at the insolence of this seminarian.

"Paul transplanted his misunderstanding of Jesus' message to Roman territory, and it became the law of the land," Michael countered.

"Mr. Dennis, St. Paul was responsible for Christianity taking hold in the European world. Christianity is built on Paul's teachings."

"Do you think Paul preached Jesus' true message?"

"Yes, and I have heard enough of your thesis to determine your grade. Class is dismissed." Father Quinn and the other priest left the classroom. The sound of fifty seminarians breaking into conversation at one time was deafening. Michael Dennis just sat at the table in the front of the room staring at his notes.

"I told you!" Michael heard. He looked up to see David Owens' face. "I told you he would flunk you. He flunked me last year for way less than what you said. But, I thought your argument made a lot of sense."

"Thanks, David." Michael collected his things and made his way toward the door.

CHAPTER SIX

Grant Sherman walked away from the rectory of St. Peter and Paul Catholic Church in Brooklyn. As he had feared, Father Francis Faye had retired as pastor. According to the woman who had answered the door, Father Faye was living in a retirement home for priests up in Westchester County. It would take him at least an hour to get there.

Mark O'Shay was looking into the reason for Father Quinn's transfer from Boston to I.C. for Grant. The fact that there was nothing in the file made the detective suspicious. If the reason was something embarrassing to the church, Grant doubted that even Mark O'Shay would be able to find it.

Grant steered his purple PT Cruiser onto the northbound lanes of the Brooklyn-Queens Expressway, which would take him past the Brooklyn Bridge to the Long Island Expressway. From the L.I.E., he would take the Whitestone Bridge to the Hutch, as New Yorkers referred to the Hutchinson River Parkway, which runs from the Bronx all the way to Connecticut. He was looking for a place called Saxon Woods, off Mamaroneck Road near Scarsdale.

The trip took him over two hours, due to a wreck on the L.I.E. As Grant pulled into the visitor's parking place at St. Sophia's Retirement Home on Saxon Woods Road near a lavishly green golf course, he was worn out and had to find a restroom. Grant had called ahead from his cell phone, so Father Faye was expecting him.

A custodian in the entry foyer directed Grant to the men's room. Once relieved, he made his way to the front desk and asked for Father Francis Faye.

"He is waiting for you in the day room just down the main hallway, sir," replied the rotund woman with short black hair at the desk, pointing to her right.

"Thank you," Grant said with a smile. *Finally!*

There were about ten elderly men in the day room, all with gray hair, glasses, and dressed in black. Grant decided to wait for Father Faye to see him and come forward. One of the elderly gentlemen made eye contact with Grant and began walking unsteadily toward him. The priest had large, alert eyes and a friendly smile of white false teeth.

"You must be the detective from the archdiocese. I'm Father Faye."

"Grant Sherman. Thank you for seeing me."

"Oh, the pleasure is all mine. There aren't many important things going on up here. I am intrigued. Please, sit down." Grant took a seat at a card table, as did the priest.

"As I said on the phone, I was hired by Monsignor Franklin at the Seminary of the Immaculate Conception."

"Yes, I know Andy Franklin, we played bridge together for years." Grant was surprised to hear Monsignor Franklin referred to as Andy. "What has he got you looking into?"

"Do you recall a priest named Paul Quinn who served with you at St. Peter and Paul about twenty years ago?"

"I remember all the priests who served with me, Mister Sherman. I remember Father Quinn quite well. He was new to the priesthood back then and a little immature. He only stayed at St. Peter and Paul a few years."

"I know, that is why I am here," Grant said. "Do you know why he asked to be transferred?" Grant took out the letters written by Father Quinn and the one supporting the transfer signed by Father Faye. "Can you shed some light on the reason behind these requests for transfer?" He handed the priest the letters.

"Oh, so you know about his requests. Father Quinn was upset by something."

"That is what I figured. I was hoping you could tell me what it was."

"Have you spoken to Father Quinn about it?"

"Not yet, but I have found in my line of work that a person will not want to admit something that is personally embarrassing. I wanted to get the story from you first."

"I don't know if you should call it embarrassing," Father Faye said. "It was more strange than anything." Grant said nothing, hoping the priest would continue. "He was getting strange letters in the mail."

"What kind of letters?" Grant asked.

"Well, that was the strange part. They were just pictures."

"Pictures? Of What?"

"They were black and white drawings of a demon."

"A demon? Good grief! This just keeps getting weirder and weirder."

"I told you it was strange. The demon had three heads, a bull, a ram, and a regular demonic head. Its feet were like a rooster, and it rode a dragon with a lion's head."

"How many of these did Father Quinn receive?"

"Well, when he finally told me about it, he had received one about every week or so for five months."

"So, that is when you supported his transfer?" Grant asked.

"Yes, I thought it best to leave the part about the pictures out of it, as did Father Quinn."

"Father Faye, do you know what this picture of the three-headed demon was supposed to be?"

"Asmodeus," the priest said softly.

"A-S-M-O-D…" Grant looked to Father Faye for help.

"E-U-S, Asmodeus is from the lore of the ancient Hebrews. The name means literally evil spirit. I am not an expert on such things. The church has tried to move on into the modern world. Demons and exorcisms are a thing of the past."

"Thank you for your time, Father Faye. You have been very helpful." Grant put the letters away, stood up, and shook hands with the priest. "Here is my card. If you think of anything else, give me a call."

"Okay," Father Faye smiled, "but I don't know much else about it."

Grant made his way back out to his car. He would drive back into Manhattan to the New York public library. Asmodeus meant something, and he was going to find out what.

* * * * *

Joseph Komkovsky walked into the doctor's office with the lunch box in his hand. Giving his name to the receptionist, he sat down to wait for the doctor to come out. Doctor Simon Gusinsky was a longtime co-conspirator as well as his personal physician. Doctor Gusinsky came to the waiting room door and invited Joseph back to his office to the great annoyance of a patient who had arrived before Joseph Komkovsky.

"What do you need, Joseph?" the doctor asked.

"You did a secret blood test last month at my request during a certain patient's routine physical. You remember?"

"Yes, and don't tell anyone about that. There are confidentiality laws!"

"I won't say a word, and you were well paid." The doctor said nothing. "Now, I want you to test this." Joseph pushed the lunch box across the doctor's desk.

Doctor Gusinsky opened the lunch box to find a vial of blood packed in ice.

"Whose blood is this?" the doctor asked.

"Three thousand just like before." Joseph answered.

"No, I don't want to do this."

"Five thousand, and I don't tell the medical board about yo

"Okay, lower your voice. Do you think your friends at the Czar can send me some more insurance clients, too?" the doctor asked.

"Done. I'll call you in a week for the results." Joseph stood up and saw himself out.

CHAPTER SEVEN

He had heard voices before, a few months ago, but he had convinced himself that it was his imagination. Now, as he had been mindlessly watching the Nickelodeon Network, a square, yellow sponge and a blue squid began speaking to him from the television.

"You shouldn't put up with the way Father Quinn treats you guys!" said the sponge.

"What do you expect?" the squid asked the sponge. "He's a loser. He won't do anything about it."

"What should he do about it?" the sponge asked.

"He should confront Father Quinn! Tell him that he is wrong to be so critical all the time!" the squid replied, raising his index finger for emphasis.

He knew that these television characters couldn't be really be talking to him. *How did they know about Father Quinn?*

"Everybody knows Father Quinn," the squid answered his thought.

"How did you know what I was thinking?" he asked aloud, which broke the chain of thought and returned the cartoon characters to their normal on-screen antics. He grimaced and turned off the television. *Perhaps I've been watching too much television. I should read something.* He picked up a book about the crucifixion of Christ. The book, entitled *The Cruci-FICTION*, supported the theory that Jesus did not physically die on the cross, but survived, which made the resurrection more like a resuscitation.

"Can you imagine what Father Quinn would say if he knew you were reading that book?" someone asked. He looked at the open door, but there was nobody there. "Quinn has such a closed mind, someone should open it up for him – with a hatchet!"

"Get out of my head," he whispered. "Leave me alone."

"I'm not in your head, I'm in your soul. If you don't go talk to Quinn, I'll start making black marks in here, and you'll go to hell for sure."

"No!" he screamed.

"Are you okay in here?" asked a voice from the door. He turned to see another seminarian, who had obviously heard him cry out.

"Oh, yeah I'm fine, I just realized I left my books in the library, that's all."

"Bummer, man."

"Yeah, see ya." *That was close.*

"Go talk to Quinn!" screamed the voice from his soul.

"Okay," he whispered, "okay, I'm going."

* * * * *

Father Quinn was in his office on the second floor of the classroom building. The door was open and the light was on. A form appeared in the doorway, which the priest noticed with his peripheral vision. Looking up, he recognized the face immediately.

"I hope you're not here to snivel about your grade. My standards are set and you know what is expected."

"I wasn't going to snivel."

"Good! What can I do for you?" the priest asked.

"I guess you can tell me why you're such a hard ass all the time.

"I beg your pardon?"

"You heard me, Father Quinn. What you did today in seminar was wrong."

"You can't speak to me like that," Father Quinn said removing his glasses.

"I can, and I will. Sponge Bob and the Squidward told me to come. They know all about you. And I can't have the little man making black marks on my soul, so I had to come and confront you."

"Oh, okay, I see." The priest was now quite afraid. "Well, I'm glad you did. You're right. I was probably out of line today. Thanks for telling me."

"You aren't going to get rid of me by agreeing with me, Father Quinn. You have to change – really change."

"Please, I want you to go," the priest said, standing up and stepping out from behind his desk. A bronze statue of St. Joseph was brought down on the priest's forehead with the strength of a man insane, laying him out on the desktop.

The seminarian ran from the priest's office, down the stairs, and outside before he realized that he still had Father Quinn's bronze statue of St. Joseph in his hand. He slowed to a walk and headed for the pond in the retreat area. Approaching the pond, he made sure that there were no witnesses. Seeing no one, he tossed the statue into the deepest part of the water and kept walking.

* * * * *

The phone rang in Grant Sherman's apartment. He awoke on the second ring and rubbed his eyes. He answered after the third ring, noticing that it was two in the morning.

"Do you have any idea what time it is?" he said into the phone.

"Grant? It's Mark. Sorry, buddy, I know it's late, but Father Quinn is in the hospital." That was enough to wake Grant up the rest of the way.

"What happened?"

"Someone knocked him on the head," Mark O'Shay answered.

"How bad is it?

"He's pretty bad. They found him in his office out cold over five hours ago, and he's still unconscious."

"What are the doctors saying?"

"He might be in a coma. They're not sure yet. There is swelling in the brain."

"How about the police?" Grant asked. There was silence on the other end. "Let me guess, the monsignor and the bishop thought it best to avoid any bad publicity."

"Something like that. They have asked the hospital to keep the priest's injury out of the press, too."

"If Father Quinn dies, the police are not going to be happy that they were not called right away. Where are you now?" Grant asked.

"I'm at the hospital."

"Okay, arrange for someone to page you if Father Quinn regains consciousness and meet me at the seminary at six."

"Will do. See you at six at the office," Mark said and hung up.

"Weirder and weirder," Grant said as he headed for the shower.

CHAPTER EIGHT

Mark O'Shay met Grant outside the office at I.C. at six in the morning. The sky was still purple and red, and the air was cool.

"Did you ever come up with anything on why Father Quinn left Boston?" Grant asked.

"Can we at least get some coffee first?" Mark pleaded.

"I guess so. Then you can open the door to Quinn's office for me?" Grant asked following Mark to the cafeteria.

"Yes, I have the key."

"I hope nobody messed around with the crime scene."

"Well, only to get the body off the desk and call the ambulance."

"They didn't use the phone on Quinn's desk to call the ambulance?"

"Uh, I think so, sorry," Mark said, realizing for the first time that there might have been fingerprints.

"And you touched the door knob?"

"Yes."

"Who found him?" Grant asked.

"Father Grissom came to look for him when he missed chapel. He goes to chapel..."

"Every Monday through Friday from seven to eight," Grant answered.

"I'm glad to see you're earning your money," Mark smiled.

"There is something serious going on here. You know that don't you?"

"Well, yeah. I mean someone almost killed Father Quinn."

"No, Mark, I mean there is some secret that Quinn is hiding, and someone knows it."

"What secret?"

"I don't know."

They reached the cafeteria, where Mark got coffee and Grant found decaffeinated tea. Mark paid for both of them, telling Grant to put his money away.

"Decaffeinated? What's the point?" Mark teased.

"Caffeine makes me squirrelly," Grant said.

"Caffeine makes me function."

They found plenty of empty tables in the austere dining hall given the early hour. Mark loaded his coffee with three little packs of liquid creamer and four sugars.

"Have a little coffee with your cream and sugar," Grant teased.

"I'm getting three of the major food groups here: fat, sugar, and caffeine."

"So what did you come up with about Boston?" Grant returned to business.

"Well, Monsignor Franklin said he didn't know, but I can't imagine that could be true."

"You think he would lie to you?" Grant asked.

"He would say he didn't know if he didn't want to answer something. So, I called around to some people I know, who know other people."

"I get it, what was the scoop?" Grant asked.

"I think there was a woman," Mark said.

"You think?"

"Okay, there was a woman – a married woman," Mark said softly, looking around to make sure no one could overhear.

"Well, that is the first thing that makes sense in this case."

"What?" Mark asked.

"That's why he was sent to a seminary – no women. Also, look at this." Grant unfolded a photocopy from a book he had found in the library and slid it across the table. The book had been called *A Field Guide to Demons, Fairies, Fallen Angels, and Other Subversive Spirits.* On page 187, Grant had found an illustration of Asmodeus.

"What in the heck is this supposed to be?"

"Father Quinn received this picture in the mail about once a week for a five-month period some twenty years ago. The picture is of the demon Asmodeus, an ancient Hebrew demon associated with the third deadly sin."

"Which is?" Mark asked.

"And you work for the archdiocese?"

"Sorry."

"Lust. The third deadly sin is lust. If Quinn had a woman in Boston, I bet he had one in Brooklyn, too."

"And someone found out and was sending him demonic pictures to taunt him?" Mark asked.

"Could have been blackmail," Grant offered, "but nothing happened when he left town."

"Maybe Quinn paid the blackmailer off."

"You never get rid of a blackmailer, besides, priests don't have money," Grant said.

"Maybe not of their own, but the church has plenty of money."

"What happened with this woman in Boston?" Grant asked.

"I think the church found out somehow and transferred him. End of story."

"Or not. These two attacks on Quinn could have been because of Boston, or Brooklyn, or something else we don't know about yet."

"So what are you going to do?"

"I am going to find out whether or not the demon letters followed Quinn up to Boston," Grant said. "You are going to find me the name & current address of this woman from Boston. Try to find out if she is still married, too."

"How am I supposed to find that out?" Mark protested.

"I'll give you ten to one that the woman was a Catholic and a parishioner, so everyone in the parish will know about it, especially if she got a divorce."

"Then you're going to go speak to her?" Mark guessed.

"And to the pastor of – What was the name of the parish up in Boston again?"

"St. Anthony of Padua. It's in the Archdiocese of Boston, but the church itself is in Beverly, a northern suburb near Salem."

"Salem? It just keeps getting weirder and weirder. If this woman Quinn was messing around with turns out to be a witch, I quit!"

"Okay," Mark laughed.

"I guess you had better show me the office where it happened," Grant said.

* * * * *

"Did you hear about Father Quinn?" asked Greg, the fat, ugly seminarian that everyone liked.

"What, did he ruin someone else's semester?" Michael quipped.

"No, his was ruined! He's in the bleepin' hospital in a coma! Somehow he got bonked on the head." Greg was very excited and his dirty glasses had slid down low on his nose again. He pushed them back up and pulled up his pants. Michael didn't know what to say.

"When did it happen?" was all Michael could think to ask his roommate.

"Yesterday evening before chapel. Do you think they'll cancel the rest of the seminar? Maybe I won't have to give my thesis."

"I'm sure they'll think of something to accommodate you, Greg. You don't sound too upset about Quinn."

"Are you? Heck, the guy was a pain in the ass of the whole world. Who would feel sorry for him? I mean, I don't want him to die or anything, but he's a jerk."

* * * * *

It was late in the evening when Mark paged Grant with the news that he had the name of the woman from St. Anthony of Padua Parish in Beverly, Massachusetts. Her name was Joanne Wheeler, and she was still married. Mark gave him the name of the parish pastor and the address and phone number of both the church in Beverly, Massachusetts and Joanne Wheeler.

Having spent the whole day interviewing priests and seminarians about Father Quinn, Grant decided to get a good night's rest and head out for Boston in the morning. He had called Father Buchanan, the pastor of St. Anthony of Padua and had arranged to meet him the following afternoon.

By the time the sun rose, Grant's PT Cruiser was already zipping through Connecticut. He knew he had to get ahead of the New York commuters or the whole day would be wasted. He listened to cassette tapes of Phil Collins and Elton John on the drive, which he figured would take at least five and a half hours. He thought about what the seminarians had said about Father Quinn. *That was one disliked priest!* While no one wished him ill, none seemed too surprised that he had been attacked. Father Quinn had made life tough for many senior seminarians, but there were no suspects that came readily to anyone's mind. One seminarian, David Owens, said he had seen someone down by the pond in the retreat area about six o'clock. Grant had yet to follow up on it.

The priest that had found Quinn unconscious in his office, Father Grissom, was of no help. He had removed Father Quinn from the office, touched the phone and the desk, had seen no one else in the building, and didn't even remember how Father Quinn was actually situated on the desk when he first found him.

Grant pulled over at a gas station in New London and allowed himself a Coke©, the only drink with caffeine that didn't overdose him. He also caved in and bought some Hostess Twinkies© to help him stay alert, having been on the road since four in the morning.

Back on the road, Grant admired the sunlight sparkling off the water of Fishers Island Sound near Mystic Seaport. Had he not been on a case, he would have stopped to enjoy the morning more. By the time he made Providence, Rhode Island, it had become a beautiful, late spring day. The only reason he didn't mind being in the car on such a glorious day was that he was making $75 per hour for driving to Boston and back, which was better than staying in New Jersey for nothing.

The Massachusetts state line greeted Grant about nine o'clock. He had not made bad time, but he was still an hour away from the town of Beverly and Joanne, the woman who dated priests near Salem. *She better not have anything to do with witchcraft! If so, that's it.* Even as he thought it, he knew he would still continue to work the case even if Joanne Wheeler was a full-blown witch. *She's not going to be a witch, you dope.*

Grant changed the tape, putting in the album "Hello, I Must Be Going" by Phil Collins, which contained the song from the first episode of *Miami Vice*, "In The Air Tonight." Reruns of the show were almost embarrassing to watch now, but in 1987, Grant had been in front of the television every Friday night watching Crocket and Tubbs. *The Bureau never gave me a car like that one Sonny Crocket drove.* He sang along with Phil as he passed exit signs for Lexington, Woburn, and Wakefield. He left Interstate 95 at the Beverly – Salem exit, which was Route 128. St. Anthony of Padua Catholic Church was off of Route 1A in downtown Beverly. Grant could see the whitecaps raised by the wind out on the water as he caught glimpses of Massachusetts Bay.

Finding the church was a small victory in itself, and it was not even noon yet! Grant decided to catch a quick bite of lunch and return to the church about one. He found a seafood restaurant and ordered a bowl of New England clam chowder and a decaffeinated tea with a little milk. The chowder was worth the wait, which was about half an hour.

At one o'clock, Grant rang the bell at the rectory of St. Anthony of Padua Catholic Church and asked to see Father Buchanan.

"Are you the one he is expecting from New York?" the housekeeper asked him as if it was a big deal.

"Yes, I'm from New York, well, New Jersey really."

"Same thing," she said with a smile.

That's what you think! Grant smiled back as the woman left to find Father Buchanan.

"Greetings!" Father Buchanan said coming into the room. He was a big man with a large head probably at least a seven and three-quarters hat size. The head was almost cylindrical in shape, with a curved face and flat on top. His teeth were always visible, and his ears lay almost flat against the sides of his head. *You are one ugly man!*

"Hello, I'm Grant Sherman, like I said on the phone, I'm working for Monsignor Franklin."

"Yes, at the Seminary of the Immaculate Conception in New York."

"That's right."

"Well, won't you sit down," Father Buchanan offered a chair.

"Thank you. May I start with a question?" Grant asked.

"Of course, I'm here to help. What do you want to know?"

"When Father Quinn came here, however many years ago, did he continue to receive any strange letters?"

"Not to my knowledge."

"He never mentioned it?" Grant asked.

"No, not a word."

"So, perhaps the first antagonist lost track of him."

"Antagonist?"

"Oh, nothing. I was just thinking aloud. When did you become aware of the situation between Father Quinn and Joanne Wheeler?"

"Mrs. Wheeler runs a small, but popular art gallery and gift shop called The Simple Things. She also goes to our church. It did not escape the notice of several ever-watchful eyes in the pews, that Father Quinn spent a lot of time with Joanne Wheeler."

"You don't transfer a priest for hanging around the gallery of a married woman too much." Grant said.

"No, but when the woman's husband comes into my office in front of witnesses and accuses the priest of having an improper relationship with his wife…"

"I guess that got around the block quickly." Grant said.

"And back. How could he stay on here and be an effective priest?"

"I guess he couldn't, but did you even bother to ask him?"

"Ask him what?" Father Buchanan asked.

"If he did it, of course."

"You mean with the Wheeler woman? Well, you see it rather didn't really matter to my situation if he did or he didn't, because everyone thought he did. So it really is his own matter between himself and God. I just needed a new priest."

"I see." *I think.* Grant said standing to leave. *I bet they called this guy "Buck" at one time.* "Then, why did the church pay out a settlement?" Grant asked as a parting shot.

"A settlement?" Father Buchanan repeated.

"Yes, the fifty thousand dollars paid to the Wheelers, why did the church pay it if Father Quinn didn't do anything wrong?"

"I'm not supposed to talk about it."

"I know. There was a gag order signed by the archbishop, but I have a notarized letter from the Archbishop of New York allowing those involved to speak to me about the matter." He offered the letter to Father Buchanan.

"The church paid the Wheelers the money to keep them from speaking to the press. In return for $50,000.00, they signed off on the gag order."

"So, everything just went away with Father Quinn."

"Yes."

"Very neat and tidy," Grant said.

"Our archbishop likes it that way, Mr. Sherman."

As he left St. Anthony of Padua's rectory, Grant was hoping that Joanne Wheeler would be an easier interview. The Simple Things, Joanne Wheeler's gallery, was not too far from the church, but far enough to have to drive. Grant found a parking place, put six quarters in the meter, and went inside. An attractive blonde woman of about forty was arranging a display of hand painted dishes. She turned and looked at Grant as he entered the store.

"Hello," she said.

"Hi, I'm looking for Joanne Wheeler."

"Please, call me Jo. Everyone calls me Jo."

"Did Father Quinn call you Jo?" Grant asked. The smile drained from the woman's face in a second.

"Get out! I don't know what newspaper you're from, but I have already said that I won't comment."

"Excuse me, but I'm with the Archdiocese of New York."

"I don't care if you're from the moon, I am not going to talk about this."

"I have a notarized letter from the Archbishop of New York releasing you from the gag order in order to speak to me. It won't affect your settlement." Grant's words took the billow out of Jo's sails.

"Oh," she said. "What's going on?"

"Father Quinn was attacked down in New York."

"Oh my God! Is he all right? What happened?"

"He's in the hospital, but the church is trying to sit on the details. Let's try to keep it between us."

"Okay, what do you want from me?"

"How did you first meet Father Quinn as a friend?"

"At bingo. He wasn't supposed to play himself, so he asked me to play cards for him. He paid, and I played."

"And when you won?"

"We split the money," Jo said.

"How much did you win?"

"At least a hundred or so a week."

"A hundred a week? How many cards did you play?"

"Thirty. The other girls only played twenty."

"Other girls?" Grant asked.

"Yes, there were four of us who played for Father Quinn."

"You played thirty cards, and three other ladies played twenty cards each. That comes to 90 cards. How much did it cost to play one card per night?"

"Five dollars."

"And Father Quinn was paying five dollars a piece for 90 cards, $450?"

"Yes."

"Every week?"

"Yes."

"How long did this go on?"

"At least a year maybe longer."

"And you four ladies each won about a hundred or so a week?" Grant knew where this was going.

"More or less."

"So the four of you gave Quinn half—about two hundred or so a week from the winnings."

"That's about right," Jo said. "It helped me save up to start this business."

"Yeah, it sounds great for you and the ladies, but Quinn was losing about $200 a week. Did it ever occur to you that Father Quinn might not have been paying for the cards that you and your lady friends were playing, but instead he might be just allowing you to play for free?"

"Why would he do that? That would be like stealing."

"Yes, it would, and Father Quinn would be making close to a thousand a month."

"Oh my God!"

"It has happened in a lot of other parishes," Grant said.

"They aren't going to ask me to pay the money back, are they?"

"I'll tell you what, I don't think that St. Anthony's even knows about Father Quinn's little bingo rip off. If you tell me what I want to know, we can just let it go. Deal?"

"Okay, what do you want to know?" Jo liked how this man thought.

"I want to know if Father Quinn told you that he was being blackmailed?"

"I knew he was upset about something, and he needed some money."

"You didn't sleep with Father Quinn did you?" Grant saw defeat in her eyes.

"No."

"The visit from your husband to the church – Was that Father Quinn's idea, too?"

"Yes."

"And how much of the settlement did you give him?"

"Half."

"So, on top of a thousand a month, Quinn got $25,000 of the church's money from your settlement?" Grant verified.

"Yes, he said he needed money desperately," Jo offered as an explanation.

"And you were able to launch your business with the other $25,000, right?"

"Yes," Jo looked at the floor.

"You knew that he wasn't paying the church for the bingo cards. Didn't you?" Grant said. Jo was going to protest, but she knew this investigator was too smart.

"You said you would let it go," Jo reminded him.

"You have my word. Besides, the church likes secrets. Thanks for your help." Grant smiled. He left his card on the counter and left the gallery.

So the demon mailer <u>*did*</u> *find Father Quinn up here in Boston! It might have taken the extortionist a while to find him again, but Quinn had obviously been paying someone for something.* Grant got into his car and headed back out toward I-95 South and the Big Apple. *I wonder what happened in Brooklyn while Quinn was at St. Peter and Paul Church?*

A thought came to Grant and he picked up his cell phone. Reading a number from his notes, dialing the number, and driving at 65 miles per hour all at the same time was not easy, but it could be done.

"Hello."

"Hello, Jo, this is Grant Sherman again. Sorry to bother you again."

"It's no bother, Mister Sherman."

"If I'm going to call you Jo, you have to call me Grant."

"Okay, Grant, what can I help you with?"

"You didn't by chance pay Father Quinn his bingo money by check, so you could claim it as a donation on your taxes?" The silence on the other end told him that she had. "It's not a problem, but it will really help me to know what is on the back of those checks."

"We still have an understanding, right?"

"Of course, Jo, I don't work for the IRS."

"Well, the checks are in my files at home. I wrote them from my personal account."

"Do you have the card I left?"

"Yes, right here."

"When you get home tonight, find one or two of the checks and page me at the second phone number listed on the card, where it says pager. Will you do that?"

"I'll see what I can find and call you tonight," she said.

"Thanks, Jo. I'll talk to you later." Grant pressed the button to disconnect the call.

"I knew it would only be a matter of time until someone came asking about that money!" Jo Wheeler said aloud to herself as she replaced the receiver on the phone.

Grant was very pleased. *Now I'll be able to get into the account Father Quinn was using and find out where the money was going.*

CHAPTER NINE

The following morning, Grant phoned Mark O'Shay at his office and told Mark that he had learned something interesting – that Father Quinn kept a secret, personal checking account at a bank in Salem. Grant gave Mark the name of the bank and the account number, asking him to have the church officially request copies of the bank records as part of a church investigation into misappropriation. He was fairly sure that the bank would comply with the request. If not, he knew a few agents in the FBI office in Boston.

"Ask for all records, statements and cancelled checks for the account listed and any other accounts in the name of the account holder," Grant instructed.

"...any other accounts..." Mark tried to keep up.

"...in the name of the account holder. That ought to do it, but they'll probably want a letter from the archbishop. Ask for a rush, but it will probably take two or three weeks. Tell them to Fed Ex it to you, not to mail it."

"Will do. What else?" Mark asked.

"I'm going to go out to the seminary and do some more interviews and check out some things I heard about the other day. How's Father Quinn?"

"No change," Mark said.

"Too bad, I really have some questions I'd like to ask him. Thanks, Mark."

"Sure thing, Grant, bye."

* * * * *

The drive to Long Island was not as bad as it could have been, which in New York can get very bad. Grant found his way to the seminarians' dormitory, where he hoped to find David Owens, who had reported seeing someone near the pond in the retreat area behind the classroom building on the evening of the attack on Father Quinn.

Asking for directions, Grant was directed to David's room. The seminarian looked up from his desk as Grant stopped in front of the open door.

"You're David Owens, right?" Grant asked.

"Yes, you're the detective who was asking about Father Quinn."

"That's right. I wanted to ask you some more questions. Do you have a few minutes?"

"Yeah, I'm just reading. Come in," David said. Grant entered the small dorm room and, since David had the only chair, Grant sat on the bed.

"How did you swing a private room?" Grant asked, noticing that there was only one bed."

"The end room is too small for two beds, and I have seniority on everyone else in the dorm, so I got first right of refusal." Grant listened to David speak, but the whole time his eyes scanned the room, the desk top, the shelves, the open wardrobe, shoes, and clothes. Noticing something, Grant stood up and paced while asking his next question.

"You said that you saw someone by the pond on the night of the attack on Father Quinn, right?" He paced to the chest of drawers built into the wardrobe on the far wall.

"Yes, someone was walking by the pond about six o'clock."

"Did this person do anything? Or was he just walking? I assume it was a he?" Grant turned and quickly read the label of a small medicine bottle on top of the chest of drawers.

"Yes, it was a he. He threw something into the pond."

"You didn't tell me that before!" Grant was surprised at this new information.

"You didn't ask me," David said.

"Can you show me where?"

"Sure, let's go." David led Grant down the stairs and out the door. As they walked toward the classroom building, Grant asked another question.

"Doesn't Seroquel© make you tired?"

"How did you know I take Seroquel©?" David asked nervously.

"I took it a few years ago, myself," he lied and avoided David's question. Grant knew that the drug was an anti-psychotic. "It really made me tired. I was taking it as a mood stabilizer. There's no reason to be ashamed of taking it."

"Well, I've only been taking it a few days. It really knocks me out. I have to take it right before bed." David pointed to the pond as they approached the retreat area. "The person was on the side of the pond by the earthen dam, the deep end. Then I saw him throw something in."

"Like a rock?" Grant asked.

"No, it was pretty big. Well, I guess it could have been a big rock, but I don't think so."

"How deep is this water?" Grant asked.

"Not too deep, about three or four feet at the most."

"I wonder how cold it is?" Grant reached his hand into the water at the edge of the pond and pulled it out quickly. "Pretty darn cold!"

"Do you think it is important?" David asked.

"What?"

"Whatever it was that was thrown into the pond," David answered.

"Could be. I was wondering if you recognized the person. I mean you know everyone who goes to school here, and all the teachers and staff. You were close enough to know it was a man. You saw that the object was pretty big. Who do you think it was that threw it in?"

"I didn't see his face."

"Where were you exactly, David?"

"I was over by the classroom building."

"Had you just come out of the classroom building?"

"No, I was going to the library. When I saw the person, I thought it was kind of odd, so I stopped to see what he was doing."

"Didn't you wonder who it was that had thrown something in the pond? Why didn't you wait to see who it was?"

"I didn't want to be seen, so I went on to the library," David said. Grant looked down at the shoes David Owens was wearing, Dirty Bucks as they were called. I see you're wearing Bucks. Do you ever wear regular street shoes?"

"You mean the kind you have to shine? No, I only wear Bucks or tennis shoes." This matched with what Grant had noticed in the bottom of the open wardrobe in David's dorm room.

"Thank you, David. You've been a big help."

"You're welcome."

"I have to go over to the office now," Grant said. "Have a nice day."

"You too," David said.

Grant walked along the sidewalk to the office. He entered the old building and made his way to the conference room. Spreading his notes out on the table, he studied everything quietly for several minutes. There were just too many pieces of the puzzle missing. Grant used his cell phone to dial Mark O'Shay's number.

"Hello."

"Mark, this is Grant. Hire me a scuba diver and have him come out to the seminary today if possible."

"A scuba diver?"

"Yeah, call the local police, they'll have someone they can refer you to. It will probably cost you about a hundred an hour plus expenses."

"What are we looking for?"

"I think the weapon used to assault Father Quinn is in the pond behind the classroom building. Any luck on the bank records?"

"As a matter of fact, yes. Monsignor Franklin called the Archbishop of Boston and said that we had to have the bank account records. When the archbishop heard that Quinn had opened a secret account, he called the bank president personally. It turns out the bank president is a member of the Knights of Columbus. He promised the archbishop that copies of everything would be sent to my office by close of business on Friday."

"Wow! That's service," Grant said. "The FBI can't even get records that fast."

"It pays to be an archbishop. Oh, there was something else I wanted to ask you."

"Okay."

"I have a lot of Father Quinn's mail. Since he was attacked, I have been picking it up to hold for him. What do you think about opening it?"

CHAPTER TEN

Mark O'Shay and the scuba diver met Grant in front of the office at the seminary. Mark had a bag full of mail, which he took into the conference room and placed on the table. The monsignor followed Grant and the diver out to the pond. From two large duffle bags, the diver began to assemble his equipment. It took him longer to put the equipment on than it took him to find the bronze statue of St Joseph on the bottom of the pond.

"That was on Father Quinn's desk in his office," one of the seminarians said, as the diver waded out of the pond with the statue in his gloved hand.

"Do you think there will still be fingerprints on it after being in the pond for so long?" Mark, who had just walked up, asked Grant.

"Probably not, but it won't hurt to check," Grant said, directing the diver to set the statue in a cardboard box, which he had lined with a white plastic trash bag.

* * * * *

Back in the conference room, Mark and Grant were glad the circus at the pond was over. The bronze statue, having dried in the air, had been carefully moved to a plain cardboard box. Mark and Grant were busy opening and reading Father Quinn's mail. Using white cotton gloves supplied by Grant, Mark would open a letter, read it, and pass it on to Grant. So far, everything was routine or junk mail.

"Bingo!" Mark said, holding up a picture of Asmodeus.

"Put the envelope and picture in this evidence folder!" Grant said. "Hold them by the corners, so you won't smudge any prints."

"There's a note in here, too," Mark said. He held the note by the corner with his gloves and set it on the table in front of Grant. It read, "I'm back! It's time to pay for your sins!" It was not signed.

"We are going to have to get all these items along with the bronze statue to a private fingerprint lab for analysis. I know of one that does work for defense attorneys in New York City. It will cost you, but we have to do it."

"You take it, I'll talk to Monsignor Franklin."

Grant took the items with him and drove into New York City, a great looking city from a distance. It was only a disgusting and abusive place once you got inside the city. He fought his way across the Brooklyn Bridge and up Eleventh Avenue to West 57th Street near John Jay College. There was an Edison Parking lot on the corner, where it was only $27 to park. *I hate this city!*

Grant knew the technician at the forensic lab. He asked for all prints to be pulled from the note, the envelope, and the picture of Asmodeus. Placing the box containing the bronze statue of St. Joseph on the counter, Grant spoke.

"I don't know if you can lift any prints off this. It was under water for a few days."

"Never hurts to try," the lab tech said, making a note.

"If you pull anything off the statue, compare it to all the prints you get off the paper stuff," Grant requested.

"You got it. You want the prints from the paper stuff photographed and mounted?"

"Yes, please."

"Give me a few days. I'll call your office when it's ready and leave a message if you're not in," the tech said, taping Grant's card into his Rolodex©.

"Thanks, Jim." Grant had used Jim often enough for Jim to know him on sight, but not enough for Jim to know his name without a reminder.

* * * * *

Uncle Joseph called Doctor Gusinsky's office using his cell phone, and asked to speak to the doctor.

"This is Doctor Gusinsky."

"Do you have my lab results, Doc?"

"Yes, they're in. You can pick them up any time."

"Well?" Joseph said impatiently.

"Well what?" the doctor asked.

"Did they match?"

"I would say it is quite obvious they are a match, but I am not going to issue a report to that effect. Any expert can make a legal opinion using these results. I want my name left out of it."

"Why?"

"Because you're involved, so I want my name out of it."

"You're such a pisser!" Joseph said and hung up on the doctor. He made an illegal U-turn and headed for the doctor's office.

* * * * *

A Fed Ex deliveryman brought a box to Mark O'Shay's office. Mark's secretary signed for the package and looked at the return address. Seeing it was from the bank in Salem, Massachusetts, she knew to contact Mr. O'Shay immediately.

Mark O'Shay paged Grant, who was still in New York City. They agreed to meet at the offices of the Archdiocese of New York on First Avenue in Manhattan that afternoon. Any records showing payments out of Father Grant's account could conceivably put Grant on the audit trail of the blackmailer.

At two o'clock, Grant walked into the offices of the archdiocese and asked for Mark O'Shay. A quick call by the receptionist brought Mark trotting down the hall, his tie flipped back over one shoulder.

"Come on back, Grant." Mark motioned with his hand and turned back around. As Grant joined him, Mark spoke quickly. "I have everything ready in the conference room. I have empty ledger sheets and a calculator and several pencils. Is there anything else you need?"

"That ought to do it," Grant said. He was amused at how excited Mark was to be a part of the investigation. "The game's afoot, eh, Watson."

"No doubt! This is exciting! I can't wait for you to crack the box open." He led Grant into a large conference room with a hardwood table over twenty feet long. There were ten overstuffed swivel chairs on each side, running the length of the table. The Fed Ex box sat on the table with the ledger pad and the calculator. Mark produced a razor knife and offered it to Grant. "Do you want to do the honors?" Mark asked.

"You go ahead."

Mark used the razor to slice through several layers of packing tape and pulled the lid off the box. Dropping the lid on the floor, he stepped back and took a seat.

"Do you mind if I watch?"

"Not at all. Let's see what we've got here."

The box contained a copy of each monthly statement for Father Quinn's checking account in Salem. Attached to each statement, were photocopies of every check, both front and back, that had been written on the account by Father Quinn. There were statements for about a two-year period leading up to the time when Father Quinn was transferred and the account had been closed.

Right away Grant found photocopied deposit slips listing the checks of Jo Wheeler and her three bingo buddies as deposit items. It was also clear that Jo and her group were not the only co-conspirators in Father Quinn's bingo operation. The priest was depositing an average of $1,700 every month from eight different sources. It was always the same eight persons writing the checks. Tracing the audit trail was much easier than Grant expected. On the first of every month, Father Quinn made out a check to The Orphaned Children's Home of Salem in the amount of $1,500. There were no other checks or withdrawals except one. Just before closing the account there was a $25,000 deposit, representing Father Quinn's half of the settlement paid to the Wheelers. The balance in the account after that deposit was $28,350. Father Quinn had written a check to Amy Anderson for $20,000 and a check for $8,350 to The Orphaned Children's Home of Salem, before closing the account.

"Well? Mark asked.

"From what I see here, it appears that Father Quinn was playing Robin Hood with the church's bingo money."

"What do you mean? I thought he was paying a blackmailer."

"Only if the blackmailer runs an orphanage in Salem, Massachusetts," Grant said.

"The only thing that needs to be answered is a $20,000 payment to someone named Amy Anderson. That is obviously the reason Quinn set up the phony sexual complaint from the Wheelers, to pay this Amy Anderson."

"For what? Who is she?" Mark asked.

"Yes, those are the questions, now I have to find the answers."

"This is turning into a bag of snot! Everywhere we turn we find another potential scandal. Where do we start?" Mark asked.

"We? Do you want to help shag leads?"

"Are you kidding? I work for the Catholic Church, This is more excitement than I have seen in a year."

"Okay, you call Father Buchanan, the pastor up at St. Anthony of Padua in Beverly, Massachusetts and ask him if he knows who Amy Anderson is. I have another phone call to make."

Mark pulled out his cell phone and dialed the number as Grant read it to him. As it rang, Mark tapped the eraser end of his pencil on the perfectly polished wood grain of the table.

"Good afternoon, St. Anthony's," answered a female voice.

"Hello, this is Mark O'Shay with the Archdiocese of New York. Is Father Buchanan available please?" He continued tapping his pencil while on hold and was unconscious of his knee bouncing up and down with nervous energy.

"This is Father Buchanan."

"Hello, Father, my name is Mark O'Shay with the Archdiocese of New York."

"Yes, is this about the Father Quinn business?"

"You might say that, Father. I was wondering if the name Amy Anderson meant anything to you?"

"What does the Anderson family have to do with Father Quinn?"

"So the Andersons are your parishioners?" Mark asked.

"I don't feel it is appropriate for me to discuss my parishioners with you."

"I only asked if they were members of your parish, that's hardly a secret. Is there a problem with the Andersons?"

"The Andersons are fine people. I am quite sure they had no knowledge of any of Father Quinn's problems."

"Then why did Father Quinn pay Amy Anderson $20,000 right before he left?" The silence on the other end was so complete Mark could almost taste it.

"I wouldn't know anything about that," Father Buchanan said finally.

"Is Amy Anderson the daughter in this family?"

"Yes, she is in college," the priest said.

"Where?" *Why is he being so evasive?*

"I think you should speak to the Andersons if you want any further information. Good bye, Mister O'Shay." With that, the priest hung up.

"You rude mother..." Mark caught himself, "Of all the nerve!"

Grant had already finished his call and was chuckling at Mark's reaction.

"Talking to Buchanan is like wrestling an octopus, isn't it?" Grant said.

"What is his deal?"

"He must be afraid of more civil suits. It is impossible to get a straight answer from him."

"I bet the archbishop or the cardinal could get him to talk." Mark was angry.

"Let it go. What did he tell you?"

"Amy is the daughter of a family in his parish. He said she is at college. That's all."

"I did a little better," Grant said.

"Who did you call?"

"I called the parish busy body, the *Chocalot* lady of St. Anthony's."

"Who's that?"

"Jo Wheeler."

"Ahhh, what did the bingo lady have to say?"

"Amy Anderson is the daughter of Bill and Suzie Anderson, lifelong members of the parish. Suzie Anderson's maiden name was Heinz. Jo Wheeler went to high school with Suzie Heinz. Amy is twenty-three now, and she was a student at Northeastern."

"Was?"

"Yes, it seems she left college after her freshman year after she got pregnant. That was four years ago."

"Ah-ha, so where is she now?"

"No one knows." Grant said.

"No one knows?"

"Nope, not even mom and dad. She ran away – disappeared – poof!"

"Right after she got $20,000 from Father Quinn," Mark said.

"No wonder Father Buchanan didn't want to talk about it. I have to get back to my office and start searching for Amy Anderson on the databases."

"Why not use our computer?" Mark asked.

"First of all, your computer is probably not as secure as mine, and I need to use databases to which I have paid subscriptions. It's just easier to do it at my office. I'll let you know what I come up with." Grant shook hands with Mark and headed for the door. It would take him at least two hours to get back to Princeton, half of that time would be spent getting across Manhattan from First Avenue to Ninth Avenue, where he could pick up the snail-paced ramp to the Lincoln Tunnel. *I wonder why there is no Fourth Avenue?* Grant had crossed Third Avenue and came to a stop at a red light on Lexington Avenue. When the light finally turned green, he made it one more block to Park Avenue, where he hit another red light. He was lucky enough to catch a green at Madison Avenue and at Fifth. *I wonder if there used to be a Fourth Avenue?* There was a delivery truck blocking the street ahead. Before he could back up on the one way street and bail out, a yellow taxi blocked him in from behind. Horns began to honk and curse words drifted along the breeze with the smell of pizza slices and car exhaust. *I really hate this place!*

CHAPTER ELEVEN

Grant entered his password as he sat at his computer in his dusty little walk-up office. He had opened the windows to allow the fresh, spring air into the room. The blinds were pulled all the way up to the top of the windows, so the last of the afternoon sunlight streamed into the room. The breeze lifted unimportant papers from Grant's pressboard desk and delivered them gently to the carpeted floor.

He entered the name Amy Anderson with an address of only Beverly, MA and clicked on the "search" button. The name of Amy's father, Bill Anderson came up on the screen along with Suzie, Amy, and their Beverly street address. The names of two neighbors were also provided along with their respective addresses. Grant scrolled down the page to read all the "hits." There were two other addresses provided for this specific Amy Anderson, one at Northwestern University, the other was in West Chester, Pennsylvania. The social security number of the Amy Anderson in West Chester was provided, and it began with the three digits 030, which told Grant the number had been issued in Massachusetts. There could be little doubt that the Amy Anderson in West Chester was the one from Beverly, Massachusetts.

Grant wrote the address down, folded the paper and placed it in his wallet. West Chester is about two hours southwest of Princeton.

Since evening was the best time to find people at home, Grant pulled the windows closed, lowered the blinds, locked the door, and walked to his PT Cruiser.

Highway 1 took him through Trenton into Pennsylvania, where he picked up the Pennsylvania Turnpike north of Philadelphia. Heading west on the turnpike, Grant picked up the Blue Route, which is the local name for I-476. The Highway 3 West exit would then take him into West Chester, the county seat of Chester County, Pennsylvania. He figured to arrive about eight o'clock. He would probably have to buy a local map or ask directions to find Amy's apartment.

Nearing the outskirts of West Chester, Grant was greeted by a heavy drizzle from a sky that had rapidly become overcast. The intermittent windshield wipers were barely keeping the glass clear. Moving into the passing lane to overtake a large blue sedan, Grant was surprised when the sedan crossed over the line into his lane. Tapping the horn, he gave a dirty look to the other driver, who had a cell phone in one hand and a soft drink from McDonald's© in the other. Grant punched the accelerator to put the idiot well behind him. *Which hand are you driving with, you moron?*

Grant turned the wipers up to regular speed after pulling up to a stop at the intersection of High and Gay Streets in downtown West Chester. Taking a guess, he turned left on High Street, passing an old stone courthouse with six brown, Corinthian-style columns.

After traveling several blocks on High Street, Grant found himself at West Chester University. He recalled the information Mark had relayed to him from Father Buchanan. He had said that Amy

Anderson was at college – present tense. *Perhaps she is at college here, and I'll find her street nearby.* Cruising past the F.H. Green Library, his assumption proved correct. Grant found West Rosedale Avenue, the street on which Amy lived. He turned right on West Rosedale and went a few blocks to the 500 block, finding a large apartment complex where Amy Anderson resided. The five-story brick buildings were a prime example of bare-bones architecture. Small black, faux shutters graced the sides of every window. The concrete balcony of each apartment was only big enough for two people if they were both standing. Large hemlock trees thankfully kept most of the buildings from being visible from the street.

Parking the Cruiser in the ample parking lot, Grant began the search for Amy's building. There were only about twenty apartments per building, so the only difficult task was to find the right building in the dark. After three or four minutes, he found the building and apartment 4, which was on the ground floor. Before knocking, he listened at the door and heard the television. *Someone is home.* He knocked three times and waited.

The girl that answered the door was wearing cut off sweat pants, a long sleeved, purple, West Chester University T-shirt, and no shoes.

"Hello, I'm Grant Sherman," he said with a smile.

"Oh, I thought you were the pizza guy."

"Sorry, are you Amy?"

"No, I'm Katie, her roommate. Can I tell her why you were here?"

Smart girl! "Actually you can." Grant showed Katie his New Jersey private detective's license and his membership card from the

Society of Former Special Agents of the FBI, which actually did more in most cases than the PI's license. "I am working on behalf of someone Amy knows from back in Boston, and I need to speak with her."

"Wow, a real detective! Are you like those guys on T.V.?" Katie asked.

"Not really. When do you expect her back? I can come back later, if that's okay."

"She's at a night class, but she should be back by nine."

"Please tell her I was here and give her my card. I will come back after nine, but not too much after nine." He wanted to speak to Amy, but didn't want to be rude.

"Okay I'll tell her," Katie said. Grant turned to leave and almost ran into the pizza deliveryman. He decided to sit in his Cruiser and wait for Amy to come home.

At about nine o'clock, a twenty something young woman walked across the wet asphalt parking lot to the apartment that Grant was watching and let herself in with a key. Grant aimed a parabolic microphone, which looked like a six-inch satellite dish mounted on a pistol grip, at the sliding glass door of Amy and Katie's apartment. The door was ajar about three inches to allow for fresh air, but it was blocked from being opened further by a sawed-off broom handle. Placing a small earphone in his ear, Grant listened to the conversation between the roommates.

"Hey, some private investigator was here looking for you."

"A private investigator! Shit! He's probably working for my dad. You didn't tell him I lived here, did you?"

"Well, kind of, but he said he was working for someone you know back in Boston," Katie said in her own defense.

"I know my father, and he lives in Boston. What else could this be about? The bastard kicks me out of the house, disowns me, won't pay for my college, and now he's spying on me? Damn it all!"

"He said he'd be back at nine," Katie said.

"Well, I won't be here. Tell him I didn't come back."

"You know he'll just keep trying. Why not just talk to him?"

"No!" Amy left the apartment and started walking back toward the campus. Grant yanked the earphone out of his ear and dropped the parabolic mic to the floorboard. He hit the lock button as he slammed the door and caught up to Amy in about 30 seconds. She wasn't aware that he was coming up behind her, so he spoke from a safe distance.

"Father Quinn needs me to talk to you," he said. He was taking a chance, but he didn't think Amy Anderson was a blackmailer. Amy spun around to face him with her hand to her chest.

"Oh my God! You scared me!" she said loudly.

"I am not working for your father. I need to talk to you about Father Quinn. He's in a little trouble."

"What about Father Quinn? He's one of the few decent people I knew in Boston."

"He was attacked, twice. I'm trying to find out why."

"Attacked? Is he okay?"

"He's been in a coma for almost a week," Grant said. "The archdiocese thinks he might have stolen the $20,000 he gave to you. I am trying to find out what happened, so I can figure out who might have attacked Father Quinn." Grant was speaking fast, trying to convince Amy to speak to him. He was afraid she would run at any moment.

"Stolen?" she repeated. "Father Quinn wouldn't have stolen the money. He's a priest!"

"Can you tell me about how you came to know Father Quinn and why he gave you the money? Please?" The drizzle had begun again.

"Let's get out of the rain," Amy said. "Do you have I.D.?"

"Sure, do you want to go to your apartment or to a public place?" He produced his P.I. license and his Society of Former Special Agents of the FBI membership card.

"Let's go back to my place, Katie is there. I thought for sure you were working for my dad."

"No, I'm actually being paid by the church in New York."

Back in the apartment, Amy and Katie sat on the couch and Grant sat in a stuffed chair ninety degrees to their right. Katie had turned off the television and turned on several lights.

"Where do you want to start?" Amy asked.

"How you became friends with Father Quinn," Grant suggested.

"It's kind of a long story."

"Start at the beginning and take your time," Grant encouraged.

"When I was a freshman at Northeastern University back in Boston, I was dating a guy who was a senior. Of course, my parents didn't approve of me dating someone older. They wanted me to concentrate on my schoolwork. Anyway, I got pregnant. Todd, that's the guy I was dating, refused to accept any responsibility for the baby. He said all the wrong things including asking if I was sure he was the father."

"Nice," Katie said with sarcasm.

"I decided not to tell my parents and just get an abortion," Amy continued. "I went to this clinic in Boston, and Father Quinn was protesting out in front. I didn't recognize him until he grabbed my arm. He asked what I was doing. What could I say? I was going into an abortion clinic. I was like – busted! Father Quinn pleaded with me to give the baby up for adoption. I told him about my father, who would disown me if he found out I was pregnant. Father Quinn asked me to sleep on it and come to see him the next morning at St Anthony's."

"And you did?" Grant asked.

"Yes, the next morning – like he asked. I told him that in order to have the baby and give it up for adoption, I would have to have enough money to live on my own. I knew my father would kick me out of the house and stop paying for my school."

"Which he did?" Grant asked, already knowing the answer.

"My father has cut me off completely. He makes Joan Crawford look like Mrs. Brady. Anyway, Father Quinn said that I would be able to get money from the Orphaned Children's Home of Salem if I gave up my baby for adoption through them. He also said he would find a way to pay for my college after the baby was born. He just didn't want me to terminate the pregnancy."

"So you started taking money from the orphanage?"

"Only when I was far enough along to start showing. Then I told my mom and left. The Orphaned Children's Home gave me a small apartment to stay in and money to live on. I had the baby, and Father Quinn gave me $20,000 for me to start over at another college."

"So you came here to West Chester University," Grant said.

"Yes. It's a nice little place, with not much chance of meeting anyone I know from back home."

"And your parents don't know where you are?" Grant asked.

"I told Father Quinn to make sure my mother knew I was going to college, but not where I was."

"It's sad," Katie said.

"It's like Father Quinn said, I had to make the sacrifice and tell the truth to my family in order to save my soul and the life of my baby. It is my father who is the cause of the sadness."

"Has Father Quinn always been so vocal about abortion?" Grant asked.

"He was a priest at St. Anthony of Padua for as long as I can remember. He always helped any girl who got in trouble like I did. Everyone knew he had a great deal of understanding that way. He never gave me the guilt trip, you know? He just understood and didn't blame me."

"Like he had been there himself?" Grant suggested.

"Well, yes," Amy said, "but I know that's impossible. He's a priest."

Grant wondered how possible it was. He thanked Amy for her help and said goodbye to Katie. As Grant began the drive back to Princeton, New Jersey, he placed the new pieces of the puzzle into his theory. *If Father Quinn had gotten into similar trouble while he was at St Peter and Paul in Brooklyn, it would explain his crusade for unwanted babies.* Grant wondered if Father Quinn was such an advocate for pregnant teens and unborn babies when he first arrived at St. Peter and Paul Catholic Church in Brooklyn. He would have to speak to the former pastor, Father Francis Faye, again.

Grant turned on the dome light of the Cruiser, took out a yellow legal pad, and wrote a "To Do" list for himself. The first item was, "Call Father Faye at retirement home in NY." This was followed by, "Call fingerprint lab in NYC to check for results." Grant's eyes darted back and forth from the road to the legal pad and back while he wrote. *At least I am keeping one hand on the wheel!* He remembered the driver of the weaving, blue sedan with the cell phone and a soft drink. *Things will sure be easier when Father Quinn wakes up!*

Grant's pager chirped. He had to remove it from his belt in order to read the number, which he quickly recognized as Mark O'Shay's cell phone. Again Grant's eyes alternated between the road and what he was doing in the car. He managed to press the correct numbers into the phone and hit the send key. Placing the phone to his ear, he heard the call go through.

"Hello?" Mark was obviously excited.

"Mark, it's Grant. What's…" But Mark cut him off.

"Father Quinn is dead! You better come."

"Are you at the hospital?" Grant asked.

"Yes. They think someone messed with his I.V."

"You mean a third attack?" Grant said.

"This one was murder."

"It will take me at least three and a half to four hours to get there, I'm in Pennsylvania."

"I'll be here," Mark said.

CHAPTER TWELVE

The Suffolk County Police were at the hospital when Grant arrived at nearly one in the morning. *This has been a long day.* Mark had obviously explained the gist of the Father Quinn matter to one of the detectives, who was eager to learn everything Grant Sherman had done on the case.

"Detective Brown, this is Grant Sherman, our private detective," Mark said making the introduction. "Grant, this is Detective Kevin Brown of the Suffolk County Police Department."

"Homicide Division," Detective Brown added.

"What happened to Father Quinn?" Grant asked.

"The medical examiner's report won't be ready until tomorrow, but why don't you let me ask a few questions first?" Detective Brown suggested.

"I told them you guys wouldn't like it that the attacks on Father Quinn weren't reported," Grant said, shooting a glare at Mark O'Shay.

"I want to know everything you know about Father Quinn if it takes all night," Detective Brown said as he led Grant to an empty waiting area for the interview. Another policeman led Mark O'Shay down the hall to a different room.

There were things that Grant did not want the police to know, one of which was that he and Mark had opened Father Quinn's mail prior to his death without permission. Grant also felt like protecting Amy Anderson from unnecessary questioning from the police. He was quite sure that she had been telling him the truth, and that she was not involved in any blackmail. As he obfuscated his way through Detective Brown's questions, Grant realized that he was sounding a lot like Father Buchanan, and it was Detective Brown who was wrestling an octopus. Grant felt now that he understood the pastor of St Anthony's in Beverly a little better. Grant thought about the bank records and the second to last check from Father Quinn's bank account. It was the only link to Amy Anderson, but Mark O'Shay had those records. He hoped Mark would not be too talkative. Grant also hoped Mark was aware of the trouble the two of them could be in for opening the priest's mail. *I hope he keeps his mouth shut!*

"I said is there anything else you can think of to tell me?" Detective Brown repeated with irritation.

"No, sorry, I'm still in shock about Father Quinn dying and all. Can we find out the cause of death?" Grant asked.

"With all due respect, Mister Sherman, you are a civilian. This is a murder investigation, in which you have no role."

Grant didn't feel any due respect in the detective's tone and was glad he had not told the detective everything he knew. As soon as he was allowed to leave, he walked down the hall looking for Mark. Quickly pulling his cell phone, Grant dialed Mark's cell phone number.

"Hello, this is Mark."

"Don't tell him about Quinn's mail," Grant said and hung up.

"Okay, honey, I won't forget. I'm kind of busy right now. I'll call you back later," Mark said into a dead phone. "I'm sorry, officer, what was the question?"

"It's detective, I'm not an officer. It's Detective Kerr. I was asking you if you had heard about any threats made to Father Quinn. Were there any strange phone calls, anything like that?"

"No, nothing like that."

"Okay, we'll send a squad car over to your office to pick up those bank records you have from Father Quinn's account."

"Fine, I'll be there first thing tomorrow morning, but it seemed to be all charity stuff – to an orphan home in Salem."

"We'll have a look at it. Thank you, Mister O'Shay."

Mark walked down the hallway of the hospital and came face to face with Grant.

"You didn't need to call," Mark said. "I wasn't going to admit to tampering with someone's mail. I didn't name Amy Anderson either, but they are picking up the bank records tomorrow."

"Let's go there now and make a withdrawal from Father Quinn's account," Grant said.

"The second to last check?" Mark guessed.

"Amy Anderson is an innocent victim in this. Why should her life get thrown into an upheaval again? Let's take your car. We can slip one page into my briefcase."

"Okay it's the black Saab over there. Hey is this illegal?"

“It’s not as illegal as opening Father Quinn’s mail. Besides, the police can subpoena their own set of records if they want, and besides, I didn’t particularly like Detective Brown’s attitude.”

“Really, Mister Sherman?” Mark imitated the detective’s condescending tone.

“Yes, Mister O’Shay, and by the way, don’t leave town.” Grant was smiling.

The drive to Mark’s office didn’t take long. Mark went in and returned with the photocopies of the front and back of the check for $20,000 to Amy Anderson.

“How much time are we buying her?”

“Never know. They might find out who killed Quinn before they even realize there’s a check missing,” Grant said.

“Did you actually speak to Amy Anderson?”

“Yeah, she needed the money to leave town and have a baby. Father Quinn didn’t want her to abort it, and the girl’s father disowned her. It was just more Robin Hood charity by Father Quinn.”

“With money embezzled from the Catholic Church!” Mark said a little indignant. “Stealing from the church can never be justified!”

“Charity is charity, no matter where the money comes from,” Grant said.

“Where was she living?”

“Does it really matter, Mark?”

“Oh, by the way,” Mark changed the subject. “I told the police about the bronze statue in the pond, since half the school saw the diver bring it out. Maybe you can go get it from the independent lab tomorrow and bring it back out here to the detectives."

"Okay. I'll take it to them tomorrow," Grant said.

"And you can check on the progress of finding any prints on the demon letter," Mark added.

"Exactly, but first I'm going home to get some sleep. I'll call you after I deliver the statue to the cops. You gonna be in your office?"

"Yeah. I'll be waiting for your call."

"You know any young priests who can keep their mouth shut?" Grant asked.

"I know a few."

"I have an idea. I'll tell you about it tomorrow."

* * * * *

Grant's eyes protested against the morning sunlight that sneaked into his bed through the cheap, mini blinds. *It can't be morning already I just went to sleep!* A glance at the alarm clock told him it was not only morning it was already nine thirty! He decided to save time by not shaving. By ten o'clock, he was on the road in jeans and a golf shirt, hoping to make the lab in Manhattan before noon.

The lab tech had Grant's results waiting for him. As he had expected, the bronze statue was devoid of prints. There had been prints on two of the paper items. Prints from the same set of four fingers from what appeared to be a right hand were found on the envelope, and the typed note. The technician had lifted the prints and mounted them beautifully on evidence cards. He had also photographed the whole process and written a detailed report and chain of custody evidence log. Grant signed and dated it, noting the time he was taking possession of the fingerprint evidence.

"Can you invoice my company, Jim? That's Sherman & Associates, it's in your Rolodex©."

"Yeah, sure."

"Thanks, Jim."

With the fingerprints secured in his briefcase, Grant made his way to the Suffolk County Police Department out on the island. He had a bronze statue to deliver to Detective Brown. Thankfully, Brown wasn't in when he got there, so Grant left the statue with the desk sergeant and headed back to the city and Mark O'Shay's office at the Archdiocese of New York on First Avenue. The trip from Manhattan to Suffolk and back took almost two hours. Grant called Mark and said he was on his way.

Pulling the PT Cruiser into a pay lot, Grant took a receipt from the attendant.

"I'll be back about 4:30," Grant said to the attendant and began walking the few blocks to the main office of the archdiocese.

Grant announced himself to the receptionist and sat down to wait for Mark to appear in the hallway. It was only a few minutes, but it seemed like fifteen before he heard Mark speak his name.

"Grant, hello. Come on back."

"We have two things to arrange," Grant said softly as they walked together down the hall to Mark's office.

“I know you wanted a priest we can trust. I have someone in mind, but can you tell me what you have planned?” Mark closed his office door behind them.

“First, we need to send a priest into the morgue.”

“The morgue?”

“Yeah, he can say he is making the funeral arrangements for Father Quinn, or some such line. Perhaps he needs to coordinate with the funeral home, so he can ask when the body will be released, you know.”

“Okay…”

“Then, with one of the assistants, not the chief medical examiner, he can start to shoot the breeze and eventually ask what was the cause of death.”

“You think they’ll tell him?” Mark asked.

“The guys in the morgue can never keep their mouths shut, and they won’t see any harm in talking to a priest about another priest. I think it will work.”

“Fine. I’ll send someone over tonight. What else are we doing?”

“I know a guy who worked as a New York City detective for twenty years. He’s retired now, but he can get someone in the NYPD to send these fingerprints to the FBI lab for comparison checks.”

“How long will that take?” Mark asked.

“I can ask him to expedite it, but it all depends on how soon they find the match, if any. It’s a crap shoot.”

“So are you going to call your retired police buddy?”

"I already have. He works out of an office over on Fifth Avenue, supplying armed guards. I have a meeting with him in half an hour. I thought I would walk over there from here. You contact the priest you had in mind for the morgue operation."

"I'll handle it. I'll call you if I get something."

"Thanks, Mark."

CHAPTER THIRTEEN

The new instructor of the senior seminar at the Seminary of the Immaculate Conception greeted his class. All of the students already knew the priest, who was currently teaching other classes at the seminary.

"I will continue with the thesis presentations as scheduled for the remaining few who have not yet presented. I have found Father Quinn's grade book and will read the final scores for those who have already presented." There were muted whisperings among the seminarians, who for the most part dreaded what they were about to hear. The priest continued. "John Adler… C+, Doug Boyce… C, Michael Dennis… A…" The whispers exploded around the room all at once.

"An A?" asked one seminarian.

"Quinn gave someone an A?" asked another. Michael sat in stunned silence.

"Okay, okay," the priest admonished his class. "Let me finish." He read off all the grades, but Michael's was the lone A, and there was only one B. Several students had failed including David Owens, who was not in the classroom.

"Has anyone seen Mister Owens?" the priest asked.

"He had a doctor's appointment," Michael's roommate answered, pushing his dirty glasses back up his nose. He turned to Michael and whispered. "I haven't seen him since yesterday. Have you?"

"No."

After class, the seminarians returned to the dormitory hall. As Michael opened his door, someone yelled from the end of the hall.

"Call 911! We need an ambulance! Hurry!" Michael ran down the hall toward the voice. There he saw David Owens face down on the floor in a pool of his own vomit and an empty bottle of Seroquel© on the floor beside him.

* * * * *

"It's an anti-psychotic," Detective Brown said to his partner. "If he was taking this many milligrams per day, he must have been being treated for schizophrenia. Make a note of the doctor's name and phone number from the bottle. We'll need to find out about this Owens kid."

"Wasn't this the same kid who saw the statue being thrown into the pond after the second attack on the priest?" Detective Kerr asked his partner.

"I think this guy was wacko enough to bash the priest's head in. It sure is a coincidence that he was the witness to the disposal of the weapon and then he kills himself after the priest gets wacked at the hospital."

"You thinking murder-suicide?"

"It makes sense. The priest had just flunked the Owens kid for the second time, the Owens kid is psychotic, he probably felt persecuted," Detective Brown said. "Let's talk to his doctor, but there is plenty of motive and circumstantial evidence."

* * * * *

Grant's retired NYPD detective walked into Midtown North Precinct and sat down with his friends in the squad room.

"Hey Frank! How you doin'?" he heard, and a hand patted his shoulder. He was offered a white Styrofoam© cup. Frank Monday stirred disgusting, cheap powdered creamer into coffee that was stronger than the odor of the restrooms at the Port Authority Bus Terminal. There were some jokes and laughs before the conversation inevitably turned to casework.

"So, what do you guys have going?" Frank asked.

"The usual," one of his friends answered, "three homicides, twenty or so holdups, and a hundred drug cases."

"You working homicide now, Charlie?" Frank asked.

"Yeah, I moved over four months ago."

"Congratulations, the big time!" Frank smiled. "I gotta run, guys. It was good seein' yas." He walked over to Charlie on his way out and whispered something. Charlie followed Frank out of the squad area.

"Yeah, Frank. What is it?"

"You got any prints goin' to the FBI for ident?"

"Yeah, I'll probably be sending some off this week." Charlie was not stupid, and he owed Frank about ten favors.

"You got a card?" Charlie asked. Frank pulled a white card with copies of the four mounted fingerprints from Grant's demon letter. He handed the card to Charlie and walked out.

* * * * *

Grant picked up the phone in his office and dialed the number of the retirement home for Catholic priests up near Scarsdale. When the operator answered, Grant asked to speak to Father Francis Faye, the former pastor of St. Peter and Paul Church in Brooklyn.

"I'll page him, sir."

"Thank you," Grant said. He was on hold for several minutes before an aged, but friendly voice spoke into the phone.

"Hello?"

"Father Faye, this is Grant Sherman. I visited you a while back to talk about Father Quinn."

"Ah, yes, Mister Sherman. Terrible news about Paul!"

"Yes, terrible news. Can I ask you something about Father Quinn?" Grant asked.

"Of course, anything to be of help."

"When he was at your parish, was Father Quinn an abortion protester?"

"No, he never mentioned anything like that to me."

"Did he work at any orphanages?"

"No, nothing like that. Is it important?"

"I really don't know yet, Father Faye. Thank you."

"You're welcome, Mister Sherman. Good bye."

"Good bye." Grant set the phone back in its cradle, but it rang as soon as his hand left it.

"Hello, Sherman & Associates, Grant Sherman speaking."

"Grant, it's Mark."

"Hey, what have you got?"

"It worked just like you said. The guy at the morgue said that someone had injected motor oil into Father Quinn's I.V. tube. When the oil reached his heart and coated the valves, he died of a heart attack."

"Motor oil!" Grant repeated, "That's an old Nazi death squad trick. They executed thousands of people in Poland that way during World War II. After receiving an injection of motor oil, the victim had just enough time to walk to his own grave."

"The guy at the morgue said the killer gave Father Quinn just enough oil to stop the heart. The police sent the I.V. tubing to the FBI for fingerprint analysis."

"Anything else?" Grant asked.

"The police also grabbed the needle disposal box off the wall in the hospital room. They think the killer might have dropped the oil syringe in there."

"If the killer left the syringe in there, it isn't likely to have any fingerprints on it."

"If the killer was David Owens, like the police believe, he might..."

"Whoa! Time out! Did you say the police think David Owens injected Father Quinn with the oil?" Grant asked.

"Yeah, that's what the guy at the morgue said. They had his body there, too. He swallowed a whole bottle of Seroquel©. They think he was crazy."

"And when were you going to tell me about that?" Grant was a little irritated.

"I guess I forgot to call you. It's been a little hectic with all of this going on."

"I understand, I agree that David Owens probably attacked Father Quinn with the bronze statue, but he wasn't behind the first attack. I also doubt he was involved in the murder at the hospital. The Owens kid was taking a pretty good dose of Seroquel© every day. He had to be under treatment for schizophrenia, which made him unpredictable and perhaps dangerous. He was upset with Father Quinn and probably went off on him. That's why he knew where the statue was."

"That's what the cops think, too," Mark said.

"But, the footprints left behind the trees by the chapel, where the first attack happened, were made by two men. Further, the shoes that made the prints were unlike any that David Owens wore. I checked his closet myself."

"So the first two attacks had nothing to do with each other?"

"I'm pretty sure they didn't, which is why I doubt that David Owens was behind the third attack. The first attack involved a needle, while the second was blunt force trauma. What was used in the third attack?" Grant asked rhetorically.

"Of course, a needle again. I didn't think of that. So you think the first attack and the third attack are probably related."

"There's a better chance of that than David Owens being behind all three attacks on Father Quinn. I think there is a better chance that all three attacks were done by three different people.

"How could it be three different attackers?" Mark laughed. "It must have been the first guys, the ones who took the blood that came back and killed Father Quinn."

"Let's just hope there is a fingerprint match from the FBI."

"How long will it take?" Mark asked.

"At least a few weeks."

"What do we do until then?"

"We wait."

CHAPTER FOURTEEN

Joseph Komkovsky was trying to speak to his sister in Missouri on the phone, but she was upset and doing most of the talking.

"I am not going to have a thing to do with it," she said.

"Why not? It's a sure thing. It's easy money. All we need to do is take this to a lawyer and we'll be rich!"

"No, Joseph, and that's final. You can't make any claim – only we can do that. You were not harmed in any way by what happened. So you can just forget it."

"The church has been paying out millions to the victims of priests like Father Quinn. I have proof, not just an allegation. They'll settle out of court, and no one would ever know!"

"It isn't right what Father Quinn did to my Nellie, but taking money from the mother church won't put things right. It was Father Quinn's sin, not the Pope's."

"Sophie, please be reasonable!"

"Good bye, Joseph!"

"Then let me talk to Nellie. She has a say in this, too."

"She isn't here. She went to visit Michael in New York."

* * * * *

Michael was in a discussion with Greg, about his roommate's upcoming thesis presentation. Greg had asked Michael to help him practice defending his thesis.

"The idea of God as Father, Son and Holy Spirit – the Holy Trinity – was created after the resurrection to explain Jesus' divinity while remaining within the idea of monotheism. It was a way to have Jesus be God and not break the two thousand year old tradition of having only one God."

"Greg, I think you should consider the idea that Jesus changed the whole religious structure of Judaism. After Jesus, the God of the Old Testament ceased to exist."

"What? How could God the Father cease to exist?"

"I said the God of the Old Testament ceased to exist. In the Old Testament, God went into battle alongside the nation of Israel against its enemies. God was protecting his nation. Heck, he supposedly drowned a whole division of Egyptian chariots at the Red Sea!" Michael said. "But, with Jesus, God the Father didn't raise a finger even to rescue his own son from death. God is now a 'turn the other cheek' kind of God – no fire and brimstone, no coming to the rescue."

"Jesus was supposed to die on the cross," Greg replied. "He died to pay for our sins."

"That was taught by St. Paul and was supposedly based on the words of John the Baptist in John 1:29. Jesus never said he was dying for the sins of the world. Besides, if Jesus was God, part of a trinity of divine entities, then no one should have been able to kill him. If Jesus was God, he had to have allowed himself to be killed by mere mortals. The crucifixion would have been a divine suicide."

"Oh, Michael! Where do you come up with these ideas?"

"Jesus was the son of God in the sense that we all are sons of God. Jesus was trying to change the idea that only healthy rich men could have a relationship with God. His whole idea was to bring God to the sick, the poor, and women – the unclean – people who were not allowed in the Temple by the corrupt Sadducees."

"Jesus created the new religion of Christianity," Greg argued. "It is built on his teachings."

"No, it is built on the misunderstandings of Christ's message by St. Paul."

"What was the misconception?"

"Greg, Jesus approached people on an individual basis and accepted everyone in the diverse culture of ancient Israel. He shunned materialism, and told people to reject phony piety. Jesus' movement was a spiritual movement for the common people. He broke bread with people that most Jews would consider unclean to show them that they mattered. Communion was Jesus' way of showing that he accepted people. It replaced the baptizing of John. In Matthew 23:13, Jesus calls the Pharisees hypocrites, because they keep the kingdom of heaven closed. They didn't allow anyone in and didn't go in themselves."

"So, you think that the hierarchical Roman Catholic Church is counter to Jesus' teachings?" Greg asked.

"Do you think Jesus would approve of his followers calling their church Roman? We even celebrate his birthday on December 25th – the traditional birthday of Osiris as celebrated by the Roman cult of Osiris. Constantine offered to insert Jesus into the existing religions of Mithraism and sun worship, and the Christians bought it. They even moved their traditional Sabbath from Saturday to Sunday, the traditional Roman day to worship the sun. Present day Christianity is more about pagan ritualism than the message of Jesus."

"You sound like you subscribe to the teachings of the discredited Gospel of Thomas," Greg told his roommate.

"Saying 39 of the Gospel of Thomas is almost word for word the same as Matthew 23:13 about the Pharisees. Matthew probably borrowed it from the Gospel of Thomas. At the Council of Nicaea in 325 AD, the birthplace of the Bible according to Bishop Athanasius, Thomas' Gospel was excluded, because Bishop Athanasius was a supporter of strict hierarchical control by the clergy, which is EXACTLY what Jesus was against. Of course they tossed out the Gospel of Thomas! Thomas directs the reader toward a simple, spiritual existence and teaches that people can have their own relationship with God without an organized church."

"We are way off the topic of my thesis, but since you brought it up, the Gospel of Thomas was excluded from the Bible because it promotes pantheism. In Thomas, Jesus supposedly said something like, 'I am all. Split a piece of wood; I am there…' or something like that. That is pantheism."

"That's not Pantheism, Greg, it's a pep talk for the downtrodden. It's almost the same thing that Tom Jode said in Steinbeck's *The Grapes of Wrath,* 'I'll be everywhere – wherever you look. Wherever there's a fight so hungry people can eat, I'll be there. Wherever there's a cop beatin' up a guy, I'll be there...' It's not a religious statement, Greg. It's about solidarity for the common man."

"I give up," Greg said.

"Okay, but your premise should include the fact that the God of the Old Testament and the God of the New Testament are conflicted personalities. It is more than God becoming a trinity in the New Testament; God abandons the idea of Israel being his chosen people in the New Testament. Jesus' teaching was that everyone was equal. The idea of a chosen people was wrong. God's attitude is so obviously different in the New Testament, because it represents the difference between Judaism and true message of Christianity."

"How do you expect to be a priest with beliefs like that?" Greg asked.

"I'm not sure I will get the chance to be a priest. I've been called to meet with the monsignor tomorrow."

"You think it's about your ideas?"

"Word has gotten around from the various instructors about my view of Jesus' message. I think the Pharisees are about to expel another rebel."

"First Jesus and now you," Greg laughed, but Michael was not smiling.

* * * * *

Later that evening, having dinner with his mother, Michael expressed his fear of being expelled from the seminary for his unorthodox beliefs.

"It doesn't matter anymore, honey," his mother said.

"Of course it matters! This is what I have been training to do my whole life! Uncle Joseph has paid a lot of money for my schooling."

"Money is not going to be a problem anymore. I spoke to Uncle Joseph today and signed some papers for his attorney. Besides, there are other churches that need brilliant minds like yours. You can become an Episcopal priest or a Lutheran minister."

"I don't know, mom."

"Everything will be okay. We will have everything we need."

* * * * *

The following morning, Michael sat in the ornate chair in front of the desk of Monsignor Franklin and received a notification that was short and to the point.

"Mister Dennis, it has been brought to my attention that you harbor certain misconceptions about the Catholic faith that I believe make you unsuitable for the priesthood. Therefore, you will no longer be considered as a candidate for ordination."

"I see," Michael said. "Am I being asked to leave the seminary as well?"

"You are being told to leave the seminary, Mister Dennis, by tonight. Good day."

"I suggest you read Saying 102 of the Gospel of Thomas," Michael said as he left the monsignor's office to go pack his things.

Monsignor Franklin stared after the young former seminarian. After Michael was well out of sight, the monsignor turned toward his bookcase and removed a thin book, entitled *The Fifth Gospel.* Opening the book to Saying 102, he read, "Damn the Pharisees! They are like a dog sleeping in the cattle manger: the dog neither eats nor [lets] the cattle eat."

CHAPTER FIFTEEN

Grant Sherman was reading the autopsy report on David Owens, which he had gotten from David's mother. She had been very cooperative and was convinced that David would not have killed himself.

"He knew it was a mortal sin," she had told him. "He was afraid of going to hell."

Grant had promised to look into the matter and asked Mrs. Owens to obtain a copy of David's autopsy report, since he was sure the Suffolk County Police would not be willing to share one with him.

The one thing that bothered Grant about the report was that a large bruise had been noted on the back of David's head. The body had been found face down. Therefore, if he had overdosed on his medication and fallen unconscious, he should have only been bruised on the face. Grant was going to have to speak to the Suffolk County medical examiner. Dialing the number from the letterhead on the autopsy report, Grant got a recording. He left his name and telephone number, saying that he was working for the Archdiocese of New York, and the victim's family on the death of David Owens.

The phone rang a few minutes later. Grant was hoping it was the medical examiner, but it was Mark.

"What's new?" Grant asked.

"This train wreck just keeps getting messier and messier."

"Why do you say that?"

"The archbishop just got a call from a lawyer representing a family that attended St. Peter & Paul Church in Brooklyn at the time Father Quinn was there."

"Uh-huh," Grant said, waiting for the other shoe to drop.

"It's a paternity suit, naming Father Quinn."

"What is the name of the family? Grant asked.

"The lawyer was hired by a man named Joseph Komkovsky, working on behalf of his niece, who was not identified. They are asking for an out of court settlement."

"Of course, that's the easiest way. What's the archdiocese going to do?"

"I don't know. The lawyer claims that they have a conclusive blood test," Mark said.

"How could they? Father Quinn is… Wait a minute, a blood test! That is why someone took Father Quinn's blood! I bet this Komkovsky guy is the demon mailer, too. Get me the name and phone number of that attorney and tell the archbishop not to settle anything."

"I'll call you back after I speak to the archbishop," Mark said. "It probably won't be until after the weekend."

CHAPTER SIXTEEN

The weekend crept along for Grant without a call from Mark or the Suffolk County medical examiner. The cold, steady rain made the days seem to pass even more slowly. If he could have distracted himself with a round of golf or a long walk, it would have been more bearable. Grant went to sleep early on Sunday night with expectation like a kid on Christmas Eve. Monday could not come fast enough, but he couldn't will himself to sleep.

It was a little past nine on Monday morning when the medical examiner returned Grant's call. Admitting that he had not looked into the details of the case in person until he had received Grant's message, the doctor agreed that the bruise on the back of the head <u>might</u> be an indication of foul play. He told Grant that he would reexamine the body of David Owens with an eye toward any further inconsistencies. Grant was amazed at the doctor's frankness, which made him seem quite trustworthy. If there were any other signs of foul play, Grant felt sure that they would be discovered. The doctor even promised to phone Grant back when he had completed his reexamination.

Mark didn't call until after eleven, saying that he had been authorized to provide the name, address, and phone number of Joseph Komkovsky's attorney to Grant. Grant was being given authority to act in the interest of the Archdiocese of New York and contact the plaintiff's attorney. Mark advised Grant that he had already faxed a message to that effect to the attorney in question. Grant thanked his friend and hung up the phone.

Joseph Komkovsky's attorney, Samuel Czarlentsky, had an office in the Sheepshead Bay area of Brooklyn. Grant dialed the telephone number and was surprised when Mister Czarlentsky answered his own phone.

"Law office, Sam Czarlentsky speaking."

"Good morning!" Grant said checking his watch to make sure he had not misspoken. "My name is Grant Sherman of Sherman & Associates in Princeton, New Jersey. I am working with the Archdiocese of New York on a matter concerning a client of yours."

"Yes, I received a fax to that effect. Perhaps it would be best if you could come to my office and meet with me in person," the lawyer said.

"I can meet you anytime you wish, but I would like a chance to ask Mister Komkovsky a few questions."

"That can be arranged, however, I may advise my client not to answer some of your questions."

"I wouldn't expect any less. How about tomorrow morning around ten?"

"I will call my client. If you can give me your number, I will call you to confirm the time." Grant provided the number and thanked Mister Czarlentsky. He would spend the rest of the day thinking of questions for Joseph Komkovsky.

* * * * *

Traffic on the New Jersey Turnpike was moving like the line for airport security checks in Tel Aviv. Grant got a short reprieve when he cut across the Goethals Bridge to Staten Island, but got stuck again at the Verrazano Narrows Bridge, where traffic slowed to a three-mile-long crawl past foul smelling landfills. *Who could live here?*

Grant was going to be late for the meeting with Joseph Komkovsky, but sometimes there was just nothing you can do to avoid it. New York traffic is influenced more by Murphy's Law than any other statute. It was already 10:10.

Sam Czarlentsky's tired eyes looked from Grant Sherman's face to the clock above a twenty-year-old, Mediterranean-style, buffet table masquerading as office furniture.

"You're late, Mister Sherman."

"Traffic," Grant offered.

"There's always traffic – This is New York for God's sake." Sam Czarlentsky didn't like to be kept waiting. "Mister Komkovsky is in my office." He motioned down the hallway past the buffet table.

Joseph stood up when Grant and the lawyer entered the room.

"Joseph Komkovsky, this is Grant Sherman, the detective from the archdiocese. Mister Sherman, this is my client, Joseph Komkovsky." The two men shook hands, but said nothing.

"If I may," Grant said. "I would like to ask two questions that might help us get right to the bottom of this matter."

"As I said before, there is no harm in asking questions. However, Joseph…" The lawyer checked to make sure his client was listening. "Don't answer until I tell you it is okay to answer."

"Okay, okay," Joseph waved his hand at the attorney.

"You may proceed, Mister Sherman," Czarlentsky said in a slithery voice.

"How was the blood of Father Paul Quinn obtained for a blood test to prove paternity of the child in question?"

"I assume there was a consent or a court order," Czarlentsky said after a helpless look from his client.

"No, there was no consent or any court order. How do you know it is Father Paul Quinn's blood that was tested?" Grant asked.

"It was his blood alright," Joseph said.

"Joseph!" Czarlentsky warned.

"There has been no controlled test done on the blood of Father Quinn," Grant said.

"You don't seem to deny that the child is Quinn's," Czarlentsky said. "We can always ask for a new blood test."

"That's the rub, counselor, Father Quinn is dead!" Grant immediately saw in the attorney's eyes that this was new information.

"What? Joseph? What the hell is going on here?" Czarlentsky said controlling his breathing. He, like most of those in his profession, did not like surprises from his own client.

"I didn't know he was dead," Joseph said. "I thought he was just in the hospital for something."

"After your client forcibly removed a blood sample from Father Quinn, the priest was attacked again. He was struck on the head and went into a coma. Later, at the hospital, Father Quinn was murdered with a lethal injection of motor oil." Grant looked at the two men who were listening to his every word.

"Aaugh! Just like the Nazis used to do," Sam Czarlentsky said in disgust.

"It will be the position of the archdiocese that your client was obviously behind the attack of Father Quinn to obtain a blood sample. From there, we can articulate a motive of revenge and claim with reasonable suspicion that your client was probably also involved in the subsequent attack that put Father Quinn in a coma. Since we already have one attack on Father Quinn by your client with a needle, it makes him a likely suspect for another attack with a needle, which killed Father Quinn, who your client blamed for impregnating his niece. You won't get a dime! You'll be lucky to stay out of jail."

"Joseph," Sam Czarlentsky said.

"What?"

"Get your ass out of my office!"

"Why? I didn't hurt the priest! Okay we took some blood – That's all."

"It was assault, you moron! And stop admitting things! How stupid can one Pollock be?"

"I didn't even know the priest was dead! The cops will find out who did this thing, and it wasn't me!"

"Would you care to prove it, Mister Komkovsky?" Grant asked.

"How?" Joseph answered.

"What have you got in mind?" the lawyer asked.

"I want a sample of your fingerprints to compare with evidence we have."

"Joseph?" Czarlentsky asked.

"I didn't do it. Take my prints! How do you want them?"

"I have a fingerprint kit in the car," Grant said.

"If Joseph's prints don't match the prints you have as evidence, it will hurt your ability to fight this paternity suit on the grounds of suspicion that my client harmed Father Quinn."

"To tell you the truth, counselor, I just want to get to the bottom of this thing." Grant unfolded a white piece of paper from his shirt pocket and placed it on the table in front of Joseph. "Do you remember this picture, Mister Komkovsky?"

Joseph and his lawyer looked down at a three-headed demon riding on a lion.

"What is that? Is this some kind of joke?" Joseph asked.

"You have never seen this picture before?" Grant asked skeptically.

"I got no clue what it even is. Are you kidding me?"

Grant excused himself and went out to get his fingerprint kit. Things were not going the way he had expected.

* * * * *

At the FBI's Criminal Justice Information Systems Division in Clarksburg, West Virginia, the Latent Print Unit conducts all work pertaining to the examination of latent fingerprints on evidence submitted to the FBI by law enforcement from all over the world. Examiners analyze and compare latent prints in an effort to make either identifications or exclusions.

In 1999, the FBI developed and implemented an improvement on their old "Big Floyd" computer. The new system is known as IAFIS, the Integrated Automated Fingerprint Identification System. Although IAFIS has other capabilities, it is primarily for searching one set of prints or even a single print against the entire fingerprint repository of the FBI. The largest such fingerprint repository in the world, AFIS, as it is commonly called, can search a database containing the prints of over 36 million persons.

Inside the Latent Print Unit in Clarksburg, the lights were dimmed, and row after row of long white tables were divided up into workstations. Each technician had a computer and an elbowed desk lamp, which could be pulled down when needed. Some technicians were entering known prints into the system with a handheld barcode reader. Others were sitting in front of split screens looking for prints that matched a suspect print to the exclusion of all others.

The fingerprints that had been lifted from the Father Quinn demon letter had already been searched through AFIS. The clerk wrote a note in the bottom corner of the card, "No Hits." The card would eventually find its way back to the New York detective with a negative report. The New York detective would pass the information on to his former colleague, Frank Monday, who would, in turn, advise Grant that the prints on the demon letter were not on file with the FBI.

CHAPTER SEVENTEEN

Michael sat talking with his former roommate, Greg, who had come to Brooklyn to visit him. In reality, Greg wanted to pick Michael's brain for more insights for his own slowly developing thesis project on the difference between the God in the Old Testament as opposed to the New Testament. Michael knew what his friend really wanted, but he was glad for the company.

Michael had temporarily moved into his great uncle's apartment in Brooklyn until he decided what to do. He was considering transferring his college credit to DePaul, a Catholic university in Chicago, where he could complete his degree in religious studies. He had not yet approached the subject with Uncle Joseph, who Michael hoped would pay for the coursework. After all, his mother had said that money was not going to be a problem any longer.

Greg pushed his glasses back up his nose and read from his yellow pad of paper.

"There is a marked difference between the God of Moses and God the Father from the New Testament. The Israelites were told in Deuteronomy 27:28 that if they obeyed God and worshiped him, they would be blessed. They assumed they would be first, and wealth was not denounced. However, in the New Testament Jesus says the first will be last. In Luke 6:24, he says, '…woe to you who are rich.' Jesus expects the Jews to help the downtrodden, even complete strangers and those who have not been ritually purified! He goes as far as expecting them to help Samaritans and Gentiles!"

"Jesus preaches that you can't just love your neighbor," Greg continued. "You have to love your enemies. The God of Joshua in the Old Testament helped the Israelites kill their enemies like the Amorites at the battle of Gibeon, where the sun stood still in the sky. The God of the Old Testament is vengeful, letting nothing pass. In Exodus 34: 5-7 God requires the sins of the fathers to be paid for by the next three generations. But Jesus claims his Father is merciful, asking the Jews in Luke 6:27-38 to be merciful as his Father is merciful. Why did this change in God happen?"

"Is that the right question?" Michael asked. "Maybe the question is whether the God of the Old Testament was even the same God that Jesus referred to as his Father in heaven."

"I don't know if we can go that far," Greg said.

"The God of the Old Testament was a creation of men who believed that the earth was the center of the solar system. In the first chapter of Genesis, there is water on the earth before God created light – It even says that the spirit of God moved across the waters. However, we know that the sun is the source of both light and heat for the earth. Unless there was sunlight on earth, all water would have been frozen solid. God's spirit would have been moving across the ice!"

"Let's not go there," Greg suggested.

"You are the one who mentioned Joshua and the Battle of Gibeon. The sun is supposed to have stood still in the sky, right?"

"Yes."

"Well, we know that the sun does not move across the sky. Rather the earth rotates. The sun does not move – the earth does. So, God would have had to stop the earth from rotating. The rotation of the earth, determines the force of gravity. The spinning of the earth affects us like a toy soldier is affected by the speed of a turntable. If the turntable spins fast enough, the toy soldier is thrown off because centrifugal force overcomes gravity. However, a non-rotating earth will have many times normal gravity, because centrifugal force stops when the earth stops rotating. All of the Israelites would have been pulled flat against the ground. There would not have been much of a battle."

"Michael, I don't want to say that God was a creation of men or that there are mistakes in the Bible."

"Okay, let's stick to your original point, which is that Jesus dares to announce a change in God."

"Right."

"In John 5, Jesus tells the Jews that his father does not stop working on the Sabbath, which is a direct conflict with Deuteronomy 27 and Genesis 2:2."

"That's a good one," Greg said, writing furiously. "John 5 – what?" Greg asked pushing his glasses back.

"I'm not sure. Look it up later. There's also the story of the adulteress in John 8:2-11, where Jesus tells the crowd that the one without sin should throw the first stone. The Law of Moses called for an adulteress to be stoned to death, but Jesus refuses to condemn her. The God of the Old Testament was very judgmental, but Jesus says that he is not here to judge anyone."

"So God is changing right before the eyes of the Jews," Greg said. "That's really good!" He wrote on the yellow pad.

"Yes," Michael said. "Being faithful and worshiping God in the Temple is now secondary to showing kindness to strangers and those less fortunate. That is the whole point of the parable of the Good Samaritan. This is why Jesus got into trouble with the high priests – he was changing all the rules. The New Testament and the Old Testament are almost completely incompatible!"

"That's not true," Greg argued. "Catholics have used both for 2000 years."

"The Catholic Church just chooses to overlook the contradictions. They, like you, are afraid to say there are mistakes in the Bible, but they are there – even in the New Testament!"

"Like what?" Greg, his curiosity piqued, asked.

"Luke 19:45 has Jesus driving the money changers out of the Temple in Jerusalem just before the last supper, near the end of his ministry. It was a defining moment in Jesus' career."

"Okay."

"In John's Gospel, the incident happens on a Passover in a completely different year. It happens just after the wedding feast in Cana – in the first year of Jesus' alleged three-year ministry. I think it's John 2:16. Well, one of the two has to be wrong!"

"Michael, you know the Bible better than I will ever hope to know it, but I am NOT going to use the word 'wrong' in the same sentence as the word 'Bible." Look what happened to you!"

"So the blind will continue to lead the blind," Michael didn't look at Greg for a reaction. "Do you want to go to McDonald's©?"

* * * * *

Grant Sherman pulled a copy of the fingerprint card from the file cabinet and sat down at his desk to compare the prints with those he had taken from Joseph Komkovsky. He held the two cards close together. It was obvious that the right hand prints were not a match. He checked the left hand even though he was sure that the prints were from a right hand.

"Shit!" he hissed. "Maybe it was Komkovsky's niece that sent the letter, or her mother." Grant would call Sam Czarlentsky and request the prints of the two women. Joseph Komkovsky was off the hook, at least for sending the letters.

The phone rang and Grant picked it up on the first ring.

"Grant Sherman."

"Hello, this is Doctor Johnson, the Suffolk County Medical Examiner. We spoke about the case of David Owens."

"Yes, Doctor Johnson, thank you for calling me back."

"I have found some other evidence that has given me cause to rule out suicide in this case."

"Can you be specific?" Grant asked.

"There is evidence that a feeding tube was inserted down the esophagus. I don't think David Owens swallowed those pills. He was probably knocked unconscious by someone, who then put the pills into his stomach with a feeding tube."

"So we have another murder."

"That is what the ruling will be. I just wanted to let you know and say thanks."

"You're welcome."

"I would appreciate your keeping this in confidence until the report is made public."

"Sure. Thanks again for calling."

"You're welcome, Mister Sherman. Good bye."

What was the motive for killing David Owens? What was the motive for killing Father Quinn if Joseph Komkovsky didn't do it? It makes sense that the same person killed both Quinn and Owens. After all, what are the odds against two people from the same seminary getting killed by two different murderers within a week of each other?

Grant knew that the motives would be the most telling clue to the identity of the killer. He thought that David Owens was probably killed to make him appear to be the one who killed Father Quinn. The real killer of Father Quinn then staged the scene to make it look like David Owens committed suicide. However, thanks to Grant, the medical examiner did not buy the suicide theory.

The only motive that made sense for the killing of Father Quinn was punishment. Someone was exacting revenge upon Father Quinn or shutting his mouth forever. *What else did Father Quinn do to piss someone off besides getting Joseph Komkovsky's niece pregnant? Well, he stole from the church, but I don't think the church would kill one of their own priests. What about the niece? I need to find her name and address and where the child is now.*

Grant picked up the phone and dialed the number of the retirement home for priests up near Scarsdale. When there was an answer, he asked to speak to Father Francis Faye, the old pastor at St. Peter and Paul Church in Brooklyn.

"Hello?" Grant heard finally.

"Father Faye?"

"Yes."

"Hi, this is Grant Sherman. I spoke to you a couple times before."

"Yes, about Paul Quinn. Terrible thing, really."

"Yes," Grant continued. "Father Faye, do you recall a man from your parish in Brooklyn named Joseph Komkovsky?"

"Komkovsky," the priest repeated. "Yes, he had some clothing stores or something. He never impressed me as being the most honest man in the world, but he was very generous. He let his sister and her daughter stay with him when they came over from Europe."

"Right, right," Grant said. "What was this sister's name? Do you recall?"

"I remember all of the people from my parish, Mister Sherman. Her name was Anna Denisov, but they Americanized their names. She changed her name to Ann Dennis. Her daughter was originally named Ninel Denisov. What a terrible thing to do to a child! You see, Ninel is Lenin spelled backwards. It was a somewhat popular name in

Russia for a short while. They changed the daughter's name to Nellie Dennis, but they moved away when Nellie was in high school."

"Right after she got pregnant," Grant added.

"Oh dear, was she the one that… I mean was Paul the one… Is that the…"

"Yes," Grant said rescuing the priest. "Father Quinn appears to be the father of Nellie Dennis' child. Do you know where they went?"

"I have no idea, but I'm sure Joseph Komkovsky knows."

"I'm sure he does, Father. Thank you very much."

"Your welcome, good bye."

Grant hung up the phone and called a man he knew in the telephone company. This contact could get records of recently made toll calls for specific telephone numbers. Grant gave the contact the phone number of Joseph Komkovsky and asked for the toll calls from the past sixty days, which was as far back as could be obtained for New York phone numbers. The contact said it would cost $150 and take a few days.

Grant was sure that Joseph had called his sister and niece before filing the paternity suit against Father Quinn. The phone number would be there. Grant would go speak to them one way or another and get their fingerprints to compare to those on the demon letter.

CHAPTER EIGHTEEN

It was late Friday morning when Grant's fax machine spat out two pages of toll calls made from the Brooklyn residence of Joseph Komkovsky. Grabbing the sheets from the machine, Grant looked down the list of many different numbers until his eyes caught a group of calls to the same number in the (314) area code. Grabbing his phone book, Grant found the area code map and found that (314) was for the eastern part of Missouri including St. Louis. Grant was making a note of the number when something leapt from the page and caught his eye. Grant recognized the phone number of Immaculate Conception Seminary, which appeared on Joseph Komkovsky's toll records several times. *Why wasn't I told about these calls?*

The phone was in his hand, and Grant dialed Mark O'Shay's number. It rang three times before Mark's secretary answered.

"This is Grant Sherman. I would like to speak to Mark please."

"Just a minute please." Grant waited for Mark's voice, but the secretary returned to the line. "I'm sorry, Mister Sherman, but Mark is in a meeting and he'll be tied up most of the day. Would you like his voice mail?"

"No." Grant said and hung up. "Meeting my ass! Something is going on, and I'm suddenly out of the loop." He knew it would take over an hour to get to Mark's office in New York, but Mark would still be there. *I'm going to find out what's going on there.*

The drive was the normal aggravating approach to The Big Apple, but it seemed more so because Grant was in a hurry to get there. He was starting to feel like a mushroom, being left in the dark and fed manure. At least it wasn't rush hour, so he was able to survive the process of entering the city through the Lincoln Tunnel without going into meltdown.

After parking the car, Grant made his way to the archdiocese office. Grant ignored the receptionist and walked directly to Mark O'Shay's secretary.

"I need to see Mark."

"He's tied up at the moment." She smiled a fibber's smile.

"Could you give me a sheet of white paper, please?" Grant asked. The secretary assumed that Grant was going to write a note. Taking a sheet from the tray of her printer, she held it out to him.

"Could you do me a favor?"

"Certainly."

"Could you triple-fold the sheet and place it in an envelope for me?" he asked. Rather than ask the reason for the strange request, she complied and handed him the envelope. "Thank you," Grant said, placing the envelope in the breast pocket of his sport coat. "Now, where is Mark?"

"I told you, sir..."

"It's Sherman, Grant Sherman. You tell him to get his ass out here!" The secretary walked away quickly and quietly. Grant waited less than a minute.

"Grant! Hey sorry I couldn't talk to you before. We have some important meetings going on about the budget…"

"Save it. Joseph Komkovsky has been calling the monsignor at I.C. Seminary."

"Yeah?" Mark's face tried to appear surprised. Grant frowned at the attempt.

"Come on Mark. What is going on?"

"Okay, Komkovsky filed the paternity suit, right?"

"Right."

"Then he says that he is filing a new suit alleging that we kicked his great nephew out of the seminary because of the first suit."

"You mean Nellie Dennis' son goes to Immaculate Conception?" Grant asked.

"How did you know her name?"

"I'm an investigator, Mark. That's what the second letter in P.I. stands for. Nellie Dennis is the daughter of Ann Dennis, who is the sister of Joseph Komkovsky."

"Okay, Michael Dennis was a fourth year student at I.C. He was let go because of his unconventional beliefs about the Catholic faith. It didn't have anything to do with the paternity suit. They didn't even know about Michael's connection to Father Quinn until after they had removed him."

"Then you don't have anything to worry about."

"We don't want this to go to trial!"

"Then you have to either pay them, or reinstate Michael Dennis." Grant said smiling. "Oh, by the way, do you have a white piece of paper?"

"You mean from a printer or something?" Mark asked.

"Yes, that would do." Grant said. Mark removed a piece of paper from the tray of the copier in the hall. "Could you put it in an envelope for me?" Grant asked yelling after Mark.

"What for?"

"Could you please?" Grant asked. He smiled as Mark absently did as he asked. "Thanks," Grant said as Mark handed him the envelope with the paper inside. "I need to write a letter later." Grant quickly wrote the initials M.O. on the envelope and placed it with the other in the breast pocket of his sport coat. "I'm going to go talk to Nellie and Ann Dennis in Missouri."

"Nellie Dennis has been staying with her uncle here in New York for the past week." Mark said.

"So she was in New York when Father Quinn was killed?"

"Yeah, I guess she was. I knew we hired you for a reason. Go ahead and speak to her. Michael is staying there, too. You probably ought to talk to him. They have an apartment at 800 Colonial Road just off the Bay Ridge Parkway."

"I'll take care of it." Grant said. He decided to drop the subject of the amount of information that was being kept from him. Someone had determined that Grant was not in a "need to know" position, even though they were paying him to find out what was going on. It didn't make sense.

The drive from midtown Manhattan to the shadow of the Varrazano Bridge in Southwest Brooklyn was surprisingly uneventful. Grant found the apartment building without much trouble. Finding a safe place to park was a different matter. The hallway of the building was dark, but at least it didn't smell bad. The elevator was a small Otis that was about fifty years old. It took almost a minute to go up four floors.

As the door slowly slid to the side, Grant saw white walls interrupted occasionally by white painted doors with white trim. The numbers were little, stick-on metal parallelograms that you can buy at any hardware store. The décor was cheep and cheesy – typical Brooklyn. Grant found his way to the right apartment and knocked.

"Kto?" came a question from behind the door in another language. Grant assumed it was either Russian or Polish.

"I only speak English."

"What do you want?"

"I am an investigator from the Archdiocese of New York," Grant said.

The sounds of the door being unlocked several times were followed by a pleasant face peeking out of a crack in the door, which was still chained.

"Are you the one who is bringing the money?" asked a woman in her thirties.

"Eventually," Grant lied. "Are you Nellie Dennis?"

"Yes." She just looked at him.

"I'm Grant Sherman, I am looking into the matter for the archdiocese. I've already met with your uncle, Mr. Komkovsky."

"What do you want here?"

"I'd like to ask you some questions that will speed things up. There are some things that need to be straightened out before you can be compensated and Michael can get back into the seminary."

"Really? They will take Michael back into the seminary?"

"Sure, you have a good case, but there are problems because Father Quinn was killed. You understand."

"Father Quinn should have helped pay support for Michael." She said coldly.

"I agree with you. I just have to figure out a few things. Could I maybe come in and speak to you?"

"Okay, just a minute." Nellie closed the door and removed the chain. She opened the door to reveal a very luxuriously furnished apartment. The couch and chairs were black leather. The rugs were Oriental and the paintings were original oils from Europe.

"Nice place!"

"My uncle makes a good living. He has paid for everything for Michael."

"Is Michael here?"

"He will be back soon."

"Have you ever seen this before?" Grant asked, unfolding a photocopy of the picture of the demon Asmodeus.

"Yes, I have seen this picture. My mother was always warning me that those who give in to lust are at the mercy of this demon."

"Sort of like the boogie man?"

"Yes this is the boogie man for my mother. She was furious that a priest raped me, so she mailed this picture to him over and over."

"Raped?"

"It was my first time, I didn't understand what he was going to do. I liked Father Quinn. I even had a crush on him, but I did not understand what he wanted to do until it was too late."

"Why didn't your mother call the police?"

"My mother lived in Russia. You don't trust the police in Russia. She was sure that no one would believe me. Then when I became pregnant, the shame was too great to admit publicly. My mother chose to move us to St. Louis and start over."

"So your mother was the one sending the pictures of the demon to Father Quinn."

"Yes, until he was transferred. We lost track of him, and the church would not tell us where he was."

"Then how did Michael end up at the same seminary where his father was teaching?"

"Uncle Joseph offered to pay for Michael to go to the seminary. He suggested Immaculate Conception to us. One day during a visit to Michael, Uncle Joseph saw Father Quinn at the seminary. Father Quinn did not recognize my uncle, but my uncle was sure it was Father Quinn. That is when Uncle Joseph decided to get a blood sample and prove what I said was true. He said we could get a lot of money."

"It sounds like you can, but your uncle didn't follow the regular rules of evidence. That is what has caused your problems. Since you had the blood sample taken from Father Quinn by force, it was an illegal assault."

"Didn't he assault me?"

"Yes, but two wrongs don't make it right. This is not Russia or Communist Poland. When Father Quinn was killed, it made your uncle's assault on Father Quinn look even worse. It made your uncle a suspect in the murder of Father Quinn."

"They killed Father Quinn."

"Who are they?"

"The knights that protect the church."

"I know you don't mean the Knights of Columbus. They might have a spaghetti dinner and drink too much beer, but the Knights of Columbus are as harmless as the Rotary Club."

"I am talking of the guardians of the truth. My mother told me about them. They are a secret order that survived when the Templars were disbanded seven hundred years ago. The guardians were begun while Jesus was alive and continued in Europe after his death. Joseph of Arimathea was one of the original guardians. When the Templars were formed, the guardians led them. When the Templars were destroyed after the crusades, the guardians continued."

"Are you saying that this group is like an underground retribution squad?"

"My mother said they protect the church from dishonor. That's why she was against the lawsuit against the church. She said the guardians would come."

"Boy, I guess these guardians have a lot of work to do in Boston!" Grant said smiling, but Nellie didn't return the smile. *She really believes her mother's fairy tale about guardians.* "Oh, yeah, can I get a copy of your fingerprints?" he asked.

"What for?"

"So I can prove you didn't send a copy of this demon to Father Quinn after he was attacked."

"It wasn't me, but you can take my prints."

"Do you have any white sheets of paper?" Grant asked.

"Yes."

"How about an envelope?"

* * * * *

Michael Dennis came home in time to meet Grant, who had him also place a sheet of white paper in an envelope. Grant marked the envelope with the initials M.D. and placed it with the other three in his sport coat pocket.

"Your mother was telling me about the guardians," Grant said to Michael.

"Yes, she thinks they killed my father."

"Oh, so you know about Father Quinn."

"I only found out after he was dead–Uncle Joseph filled the law suit."

"You know more about the Catholic Church than I do, Michael. What is your take on these guardians?"

Looking at his mother before speaking, Michael received a nod and began speaking.

"Grandma calls them the guardians, which is what they were called in Poland when she was a girl. The group she is talking about is officially known as the Priory of Sion. They have acted in the shadows for centuries, behind the scenes, orchestrating critical events in history on behalf of the Vatican."

"Sounds like the CIA," Grant laughed.

"The CIA has nothing on the Priory of Sion."

"How can I find out more about them?" Grant asked.

"You should speak to Dr. Charles Mink."

"Who is he?"

"He is Professor Emeritus in Religious and Folk History at Lincoln University in Jefferson City, Missouri. He can tell stories from history for hours."

"Is Lincoln a Catholic school?"

"No, and neither is Dr. Mink, at least not anymore. He likes to say that he was a Catholic until he got educated. He can tell you more about the Priory of Sion than you want to know."

"If he is Professor Emeritus, then he's retired. How do I find him?"

"He lives out on a rural route in Osage County, Missouri with a bunch of cows. I think I still have his phone number. You should really go and speak to him in person. He doesn't like to talk on the phone like he does in person."

"How did you meet this Dr. Mink?"

"I took two classes from him one summer. He showed me that most of what you hear from people is pure bull, especially people in power."

"What you know and what you can say are two different things, Michael. I learned that the hard way working for the feds."

"I learned the same thing the hard way at the seminary."

Grant turned to Michael's mother and asked her to call her mother in St. Louis.

"If I am going to Missouri, I might as well stop and interview your mother, if you think she will speak to me."

"I will tell her it is okay," Nellie said, finally showing a slight smile. "I think you are an honest man."

"Thank you," Grant said. "Sometimes that's all I have."

CHAPTER NINETEEN

Trans World Airlines' hub of operation is in St. Louis so finding a flight directly from Philadelphia to St. Louis was not difficult. TWA didn't partner with any airline with which Grant had a frequent flyer account, but a direct flight without frequent flyer miles was still better than changing planes in Detroit, Atlanta, or Dallas. Grant wasn't even sure that the archdiocese was going to reimburse him for this little foray to the Mid-West. At this point, that was secondary to finding out the truth. There was something dark lurking just under the surface of this case. Grant, who believed that Lee Harvey Oswald acted alone, didn't usually go in for conspiracy theories. He didn't think there was a second gunman on "the grassy knoll" that day in Dallas, but he felt the need for more information about this mysterious Priory of Sion. He wondered if Mark O'Shay had ever heard of the organization. *Why does the Vatican need a Gestapo?*

The flight to St. Louis was not unpleasant. Since there was no meal in coach, he was ignored after receiving the initial Coke and pretzels immediately after takeoff. He had picked up a book at the airport bookstore called <u>The Templar Revelation: Secret Guardians of the True Identity of Christ</u>, by Lynn Picket & Clive Prince. There were multiple references to the Priory of Sion in the Index. Grant began making notes.

"Prominent Members of the Priory of Sion:" he wrote on a legal pad. "Sir Isaac Newton, Leonardo Da Vinci, Victor Hugo, and Pope John XXIII." Grant read more and continued to make notes. "Presided over by a Grand Master, each of whom takes the name John." *Why, I wonder?*

Grant found an interesting segment about codes and clues left in the art works of Leonardo Da Vinci, specifically in *Last Supper*. According to the book, there was a clue in the painting as to the true identity of "the beloved disciple," who has long been considered the author of the Gospel according to John. *There we go with John again! I'll have to ask Dr. Mink what's up with this John business and the Priory of Sion.* Grant also made a note to get a copy of the *Last Supper* by Da Vinci.

As the Boeing 737 banked for approach to Lambert Field in St. Louis, Grant strained to try to find the Gateway Arch. *Kind of dumb thing to do, but I always look for the Statue of Liberty when I fly into Newark International, too.* He found the Arch as well as Busch Stadium and some assorted riverboats on the Mississippi River.

Grant had decided to track down Michael Dennis' grandmother on the way out of St. Louis. He was going to rent a car and drive the 120 miles to the state capital, Jefferson City, on the south bank of the Missouri River in the center of the state. Dr. Mink had agreed to speak to him in person, but they had made no detailed plans. Hopefully, the professor would come into the city to speak with him. Grant didn't want to be searching down cow paths in the boonies of

Missouri. He was supposed to call Dr. Mink when he arrived at his hotel.

* * * * *

Dr. Charles Roundtree Mink was a good-humored, elderly gentleman with white hair. He wore a shabby, navy blue sport coat with a light blue Oxford shirt and a red tie. His face was round, and the professor's glasses gave his eyes a beady appearance.

"Hello, Dr. Mink, thank you for agreeing to speak with me," Grant said shaking hands with the professor at the lobby of the restaurant on the top level of a round Holiday Inn in Downtown Jefferson City.

"Call me Charlie. Why don't we get a table? They have a good buffet here."

"Okay," Grant said.

"I have to get an iced tea, then we can talk."

A waitress nodded knowingly and met Dr. Mink with an iced tea as soon as he sat down.

"Thank you, extra lemon – just like I like it." The waitress smiled and walked away pleased with herself. "I come here a lot," Charlie said.

"I guess so."

"Okay, you said you wanted to know about the Priory of Sion. Some people call it the Priory of Zion. It was a secret organization – part of the folklore of Europe."

"So it doesn't really exist?"

"Well, not anymore, at least not like it once did. Their mission has changed several times over the centuries."

"I read a little on the plane about Leonardo Da Vinci being a member, and that he left hidden clues in his works." Grant said.

"You're talking about his *Last Supper*. The person on the right hand of Jesus in the painting is supposedly John, the beloved disciple. However, upon close examination you notice that this is the only person in the painting without a beard, which all Jewish men had. The face is also very effeminate. The clue is that the beloved disciple known as John, who wrote one of the four Gospels of the New Testament, was really Mary Magdalene."

"Really?"

"You can even see a sort of M-shape in the way the bodies of the beloved disciple and Jesus are situated. They are leaning away from each other, and it looks like a letter M, which is supposed to stand for Mary Magdalene."

"So John was a woman?" Grant asked.

"I deal in folklore, man. You sort out what is true and what isn't," Charlie chuckled. "So, Mary Magdalene is the beloved disciple. Now, according to the Gospel of Phillip…"

"Phillip?"

"It was tossed by the Church at the Council of Nicaea."

"Oh, that's why I missed it," Grant smiled.

"Yeah, Phillip has the rest of the disciples complaining to Jesus that he loves Mary Magdalene more than he loves them."

"Really?" Grant said.

"Yeah, see why the church tossed it?"

"Yes, too spicy."

"Mary Magdalene was supposedly the sister of Jesus' good friend Lazarus. Mary and Lazarus were very well off, living in a large house in Bethany, near Jerusalem. The Gospel of John is the only one that tells about Jesus' time in the southern part of Israel, in Judea. The other three tell about what Jesus did up north in Galilee. The idea is that the 12 apostles didn't always travel to Bethany with Jesus."

"Why not?"

"The group of Jesus' friends in Bethany was the beginning of the Priory of Zion. They were a group who worked behind the scenes to make Jesus appear to be the Messiah."

"Who else was in this group?" Grant asked.

"Joseph of Arimathea, Jesus' brother Jude, Simon Magnus the magician, a man named Nicodemus, and several others. You know when Jesus arrived in Jerusalem with his apostles on Palm Sunday, a week before the crucifixion?"

"Yes."

"Jesus told two apostles to go to the gate of the village of Bethany and there they would find a donkey. He told them to take it, but if they were challenged by the owners, they were to say that the master needs him."

"I remember the story," Grant said.

"Well, Jesus had arranged for a donkey to be there with his Bethany group. The stupid apostles thought it was prophecy. That way Jesus could ride into the city on a donkey as was written in the book of Zechariah."

"So he set it all up ahead of time?"

"Of course! Then you recall that Jesus told some other apostles to check about a room for the last supper?"

"Yes."

"He told them to go to the well by the gate to the city and look for a man carrying water, which was a job usually relegated to women. A man carrying water would stand out. Jesus told them to follow that man to a house, where they were to ask about a room already prepared. The beloved disciple, who was not one of the twelve, eats with them. Well, you can guess whose house they were in."

"Mary Magdalene's."

"Yep, at least according to the legend of the Priory of Zion. It goes on and on. The main idea is that Jesus was married to Mary Magdalene. Simon Magnus the magician gets himself appointed to help Jesus carry his cross. Together with Joseph of Arimathea, Simon helps convince everyone that Jesus really died on the cross, while he really didn't."

"So when Jesus appears later…"

"He was merely revived. Have you heard about the mural in the Cathedral of Notre Dame by the famous French painter Jean Cocteau?"

"Sorry, I'm not much into art."

"It depicts the crucifixion, but the face of man on the cross is not visible. One of the men in the crowd, however, has something remarkable on his face. One of his eyes is unmistakably drawn in the shape of a fish."

"A fish?" Grant asked, looking for the significance.

"A fish is the symbol of Jesus. He fed the multitudes with two fishes. He made simple fishermen into fishers of men!"

"So this artist Cocteau is saying that Jesus watched as the Romans crucified someone else?" Grant asked.

"Of course, the Romans didn't know what Jesus looked like, there were no wanted posters, saying, WANTED for claiming to be the Messiah! Besides, Cocteau was a Grand Master of the Priory of Sion."

"This story sort of spoils the fun of Easter, doesn't it?"

"Why not? Christmas is based on a bunch of made up stuff, too. Anyway, Joseph of Arimathea then takes Mary Magdalene, who is with child, to Egypt to protect her and the future son of Jesus."

"What?" Grant was thinking about the grassy knoll in Dallas again. "This is a better conspiracy than in the movie JFK!"

"I told you..."

"I know – it's only folklore," Grant repeated.

"Right. You've heard of the flight to Egypt, where Joseph takes Mary and her son to Egypt to protect them from King Herod?"

"Yes, but didn't that story involve Mary the mother of Jesus and her husband Joseph the carpenter, running from King Herod the Great?"

"That's the way it has been interpreted, but the story was told differently by the Priory of Zion. They claimed that the story refers to

Herod Antipas, the King of Judea at the time of the crucifixion, who also wants all of Jesus' family killed to protect his shaky claim to the throne. Did you know that the Herod kings were actually Arabs appointed to power by the Roman Empire?"

"No, that's another thing I've learned today."

"Okay, the members of the Priory become the guardians of Jesus and Mary Magdalene. The Priory of Zion began to refer to Jesus and Mary Magdalene with the code names. Mary Magdalene's was 'John' – the first John. Every Grand Master of the Priory..."

"I know, took the name John," Grant said.

"Right, you have been reading."

"So where does this all lead, Charlie?"

"To France."

"France?"

"Yes, Joseph of Arimathea took Mary Magdalene to France, where she raised the son of Jesus, who is supposedly buried in the French Village of Rennes-le-Chateau."

"Where did this cockamamie story come from?" Grant asked.

"Where all folklore comes from: people talking. Even the Koran says that Jesus didn't die on the cross, but tricked everyone."

"At least the Jews and the Muslims can agree on one thing – that Jesus didn't come back from the dead," Grant smiled.

"Would you like to hear the folklore behind the 19th century discovery of what was found at Rennes-le-Chateau in France?"

"Sure, but when do we get to the Priory of Sion becoming the Catholic version of the Gestapo?" Grant asked.

"That comes later. The Vatican turned on the Priory of Sion, which claimed that the Merovingian kings in France were the direct descendants of Jesus Christ, and therefore, descendants of King David and Moses. They wanted a Merovingian named Dagobert II to be placed on the throne of the Holy Roman Empire and England."

"Takes the idea of Enlightened Despotism to a whole new level," Grant said.

"Yeah, the Vatican drew the line there. The Pope had King Dagobert II killed, and the Priory went completely underground forever. Eventually, the Priory reconciled with the Vatican under Pope John XXIII, who had joined the Priory while he was in Paris as the Vatican's ambassador to France. That is when the Priory became like the CIA for the Pope."

"So they really go around doling out private justice?" Grant was skeptical.

"It is said that several of the current members of the Priory are former Irish Republican Army members. They are trained killers for the Vatican, modern crusaders."

"You're serious!"

"I don't know what to believe about the Catholic Church anymore, but when the IRA boys got into the Priory, British MI-6 wasn't far behind." Charlie said.

"It's like a Robert Ludlum novel!"

"I wouldn't doubt that there are double agents from the CIA in there too."

"And they really kill people?"

"What do you think?"

"I don't know what to think," Grant said.

"So anyway," Charlie continued, "in 1885 a new priest is assigned to be the pastor of the church at Rennes-le-Chateau. The place needed some major work, so he set about remodeling the church. The priest, Berenger Sauniere, lifted the altar stone and found a hidden compartment. In the compartment were several parchments, some over 600 years old, which gave the genealogy of the descendants of Jesus. There was also a cryptic message, which gave the location of a grave. The code was finally broken and it said something about 'a treasure and he is there dead.' Many thought that it was the grave of Jesus, but the Vatican didn't like the idea of finding the grave of Jesus. Like you said, it ruined Easter. The official version now is that the grave is that of Jesus' first son."

"Is that it?" Grant asked.

"That's a lot."

"How much of it is true?"

"How much of anything is true and how much is bull? You asked me if there is a secret society in the Catholic Church called the Priory of Zion. The folklore says yes, and it has changed and evolved over the years. However, anyone who says they belong to a group like that in the twenty-first century is pretty scary if you ask me."

"I guess anything is possible. Thank you for your time, Charlie."

"Your welcome. I enjoy getting to tell my stories to someone who hasn't heard them before. My wife has heard every story I've got."

"Thanks, again." Grant shook hands with the professor and walked out of the restaurant. He would spend the night in Jefferson City and leave for St. Louis in the morning.

* * * * *

Grant arrived back in the Philadelphia airport on a Tuesday. He had fingerprints from Ann Dennis to go with the other sets of prints. He wanted to get home to make comparisons to the prints from the letter and picture of the demon Asmodeus, which had been sent to Father Quinn just before his murder.

Parking the PT Cruiser on the street outside his office in Princeton, Grant went up the stairs two at a time and unlocked the door. The smell of an old house greeted him. It was too hot, so he turned on the window-mounted, air conditioning unit and went right to work. Laying out five envelopes, on his desk, Grant donned white cotton gloves to keep his own prints off the papers.

Grant opened the envelope marked, "A.D." for Ann Dennis. Unfolding the blank sheet of paper, he dipped a magnetic wand into some dark gray power. Like iron filings, the powder stuck to the magnetic wand. Pulling the powder back and forth over the clean white paper, Grant watched as prints became visible.

Holding the sample card from the demon letter next to the newly uncovered prints of Michael's grandmother, Grant was surprised to see that the prints were not similar. *But she was the one that sent the other pictures of Asmodeus. She admitted it!* Ann Dennis told Grant that she had sent several pictures of the demon Asmodeus to Father Quinn many years ago, but denied any recent mailings. Of course, at the time, Grant didn't believe her. *I guess she was telling the truth! So it wasn't Uncle Joseph or grandma.*

Grant opened the envelope marked "N.D." for Nellie Dennis and worked the magnetic powder around the paper – It was also not a match. The "M.D." envelope from Michael yielded the same result. Grant decided to try Mark O'Shay's fingerprints, which he had taken when he thought he was being excluded from something at the archdiocese. Mark's prints were also not a match. Having one envelope left, Grant went through the motions again with the magnetic wand and the powder. As the prints darkened with each pass of the wand, Grant's hair stood on end. The fingerprints of Mark's secretary matched the prints on the letter that had been sent with the picture of Asmodeus to Father Quinn.

Wait a minute! If the letter came from the archdiocese, then there is no blackmailer of Father Quinn. The letter was a fake! It had to be placed in with Father Quinn's other mail by someone who knew about the old demon letters. But the only person I told was...

Grant had dialed the phone number quickly and was tapping his pencil on the desk rapidly as he waited for an answer.

"Archdiocese of New York, may I help you?"

"Mark O'Shay, please."

"One moment." The one moment seemed like a really long time.

"Hello, this is Mark."

"Do you want to talk about why you faked the demon letter to Father Quinn now or in my office?" Grant asked.

"What are you talking about, Grant?"

"Don't even bother. I just matched the fingerprints."

"Of course, my prints were on the envelope, I brought the mail to you. Remember?"

"Mark, I didn't find your prints. I found your secretary's prints. It must have been from when she loaded the paper into the printer. Your prints weren't on the letter, because you were wearing gloves!"

"My secretary? Well, maybe she had something to do with it…"

"Come on, Mark, you're embarrassing yourself. You are the only one I told about the pictures of Asmodeus. You were trying to deflect the investigation toward a non-existent black-mailer from the start."

"Okay, I was trying to make it look like Joseph Komkovsky was a blackmailer to stop him from suing the church. Is that so bad?"

"You lied to me."

"But, Grant…"

"I don't want to hear it. I want to hear what you know about the guardians." There was silence on the line. "Mark?"

"Yeah?"

"What does the Priory of Sion have to do with Father Quinn's death? More silence followed. "Mark?"

"Yeah?"

"You're not saying anything."

"I can't say anything. I don't know what you're talking about."

"You are a really bad liar. Don't call me again. I'll be mailing my final bill to the archdiocese. Make sure I get paid within thirty days!" Grant hung up the phone. His mind was racing.

It was Mark's idea to open Father Quinn's mail in the first place. He knew we'd find the demon letter because he put it in there. Where was Mark when he called me to tell me that Father Quinn was dead? He told me to come to the Hospital. Mark was at the hospital when he called me. He would have called me as soon as he found out that Father Quinn was dead. If he did, then he was already at the hospital when he got the word. Why would he have been there? Did Mark kill Father Quinn? If so, then he also killed David Owens to attempt to shift the blame to the seminarian. But then Mark would have been using me from the start, trying to find out what was going on. When the scandal surfaced, he would want to put a stop to it, but with a double murder? It doesn't make sense! Why was Mark so quiet when I mentioned the guardians – the Priory? This mystery isn't solved – it is just starting!

CHAPTER TWENTY

Grant decided that Mark O'Shay knew much more than he was willing to say on the phone. He planned to be at Mark's apartment when Mark got home from work and get some answers. Grant felt sure that Mark had not been evasive as much as he had been afraid. Either way, he knew something about the death of Father Quinn that he had not shared with Grant.

The purple PT Cruiser moved from lane to lane on the New Jersey Turnpike weaving around the slower cars. At the speed Grant was driving, all of the other cars were slower cars. When he reached the entrance to the Lincoln Tunnel, Grant glanced at the clock on the dash. *Forty-three minutes! Not bad.*

The commuter rush had not yet reached full strength, so Grant was able to make it across Manhattan in only twenty minutes. Finding a parking lot a few blocks from Mark's apartment, Grant took a receipt from the attendant and trotted off toward the front door of Mark's building.

Choosing to wait out front, Grant watched as yellow cabs deposited their passengers on the curb. He was sure that Mark didn't take a cab to work, but drove his own car, the black Saab. Grant had ridden in it from the Suffolk County Police Department to Mark's office the night Father Quinn was killed. *A black Saab, there must be a garage nearby where he rents a space.*

Grant walked out to First Avenue and looked downtown at the oncoming traffic. *He has to show up sooner or later.* Grant looked at his watch – 5:15. The office of the archdiocese was not that far away. *There he is!*

Mark's Saab pulled into a garage across the street and one block up from his apartment building. Leaving the Saab for the attendant, Mark stopped to wait for a chance to cross the street. Suddenly, a blue van screeched to a halt in front of Mark. A man with dark hair, a green t-shirt, and black jeans ran up from behind and pushed Mark into the open door on the side of the van. Grant ran up the street trying to get the license number of the van. He saw it was a New York plate the last four numbers were 8011. A cab was stopping to pick up a young man and his girlfriend. Grant ran to the cab and beat the couple into the back seat.

"I'll give you a fifty buck tip, drive!" The cab accelerated away from the surprised couple. "Follow that blue van! He's two blocks up. He just turned left."

"I see him. You a cop?"

"FBI!" Grant lied. "Don't lose him." Grant pulled a fifty from his wallet and tossed it into the front seat. "I need to get the license plate number."

"You got it mister FBI!" the cabbie said. He was a short, heavy man about 50 years old with an Italian accent. "You know I always wait for someone to say follow that car. We'll get close to him."

The van picked up the FDR North at 63rd Street. The cabbie got close enough for Grant to read the full license plate number. However the van was going pretty fast, and the FDR is not a smooth ride by anyone's standards. Several times the cab's gas tank scuffed the pavement.

"He gonna take the Triborough Bridge," the cabbie said. Grant took out his cell phone and dialed 911. When the operator answered, he spoke quickly, but calmly.

"There is a kidnapping in progress. The subjects are in a blue van crossing the Triborough Bridge into Queens." Grant gave the plate number of the van and said he was a former FBI agent.

"Can you stay on the line?" the operator asked. However, the metal superstructure of the bridge cut off his signal.

"Shit!"

"He's going south," the cabbie said.

"What road is this?" Grant asked.

"278 South." The cabbie said, with both hands on the wheel. "I still see him." Grant tried to call 911 again, but he got a new operator. Telling her the same story, Grant asked her to tell the police that the kidnappers were now going south on 278 in Queens. Then he lost the signal again.

"Shit! Hey, we're not staying on 278!" Grant yelled as he saw the signs above the highway.

"Grand Central Parkway," the cabbie yelled. "He's going to the airport."

"LaGuardia?" Grant asked.

"Of course La Guardia!" The cabbie frowned at Grant. "You not a New Yorker?"

"Not really." Grant dialed 911 once more and told them to advise the police that the blue van with the kidnap victim was going to LaGuardia airport.

"He's a going to the cargo terminals. Without a pass, we gonna loose him! Show 'em your badge."

"Just keep going!"

"What about the wooden gate?"

"Just keep going, damn it!"

"You will pay?" the cabbie asked.

"Yes, I'll pay!" Grant said as the wooden gate splintered around the grill of the taxi. The security guard took three steps after them and then ran back to the little shack. "We'll have plenty of cops here really soon!" Grant said. "Where did he go?"

"He turned right at the white hangar." The cabbie copied the turn, but the van was not in view. "Hey! What happen?" He brought the cab to a stop.

"Shit!" Grant couldn't believe they had lost the van. "They have to be around here someplace." He opened the door to the cab.

"That will be far enough!" Grant heard a voice from a bullhorn. "Just stay right where you are and put your hands up." Three security vehicles were heading toward the taxi. *We'll sort this out. The driver of the van had to have had an FAA clearance. We'll find out whose van it was, and where they went.* Grant raised his hands and waited for a chance to tell his story.

* * * * *

Mark O'Shay was pulled from the blue van inside an airline hangar and shoved into another van. The man with the green t-shirt and black jeans held a small black .22 caliber pistol. The new van was brand new and white with tinted windows. The hangar door was raised and they drove back outside, where Mark saw Grant standing with his hands in the air. Grant didn't see Mark because the tinted windows were so dark.

"Grant!" Mark yelled as loud as he could. A lead-filled, leather blackjack cracked against his skull, dropping Mark like a bag of wet sand. Grant looked around, his eyes scanning. *Did someone call my name?* He noticed the white van with a New York plate, leaving the airport. *They switched vans!* Grant quickly read the plate and said the number over and over in his head so he would remember it.

"They're getting away!" Grant said, but it was no use. These security guards knew nothing about the kidnapping, as far as they were concerned, Grant and the cabbie were the problem. *No one cares about a van leaving the airport. These guys are good.*

* * * * *

Grant sat in a bare interview room at LaGuardia, staring up at the bare light bulb, which provided insufficient light for even the closet-sized room. Since there were no windows and no pictures on the gray walls, Grant had been staring into the bulb trying to read whether it was a sixty or seventy-five watt bulb. Closing his eyes, Grant saw a blue remnant of the bulb floating in the darkness on the underside of his eyelids. Having told his entire story to a Special Agent of the FBI, Grant had been waiting for the agent to return for over an hour.

Grant had not known the agent, which is not surprising since over one thousand agents are assigned to the New York Division of the FBI. LaGuardia is handled by the Brooklyn-Queens Resident Agency, while Grant had worked out of the main office at 26 Federal Plaza in Lower Manhattan. He had never been to the Queens office in all his years working as an agent in New York.

The door to the tiny interview room finally opened, and the agent returned. The agent's bushy moustache did not conceal his frown.

"Mister Sherman, I tried to check out your story, but there are a few problems."

"What? I told you I used to be an FBI agent. Did you check on that?"

"Well, I did."

"And?"

"That's the problem. I spoke to your former supervisor, who said that FBI Headquarters asked that you submit to a psychiatric evaluation."

"Yeah, they did."

"And that you told them to stuff it."

"I resigned, if that's what you mean."

"So, you can understand that we have a little credibility problem to start with."

"Just because I took pills for depression doesn't mean I don't know a kidnapping when I see one!" Grant said, trying to keep his temper.

"You told the cab driver that you were an FBI agent."

"So he would follow the van with the kidnap victim in it!"

"The license plate you called in to 911 for the blue van is not even on file."

"These guys are professionals! They already killed the priest. Didn't you call the Suffolk County Police?"

"Yes, I spoke to a Detective Brown."

"Good, what did he tell you?"

"That you were messing around in his investigation, and he had asked you to butt out."

"But I'm working on this case for the Archdiocese of New York!"

"Well, not according to them," the agent said calmly.

"What? That's impossible!"

"I spoke to Archbishop Moreau himself."

"And?"

"He said that you called this Mark O'Shay, that you claim was the kidnap victim, and resigned from the case today."

"Oh shit! You don't believe a word I'm telling you."

"Not really."

"You think I'm a nut job, don't you?" Grant asked.

"Pretty much. I'm willing to let the whole thing go. The airport security director wants your ass on a pike, but I told him there are some mental health issues."

"I'm not crazy! Mark O'Shay was kidnapped!"

"Mark O'Shay called his secretary at home about an half an hour ago and said he was going out of town for a few days. He asked her to put him in for vacation leave for the rest of the week"

"That's impossible! The kidnappers must have forced him to make the call."

"To make you look crazy?

"No, so the people at the archdiocese didn't report him missing."

"I don't think so. There is just no reason for anyone to take you seriously, Mister Sherman."

"Can I ask you one thing?"

"What's that?"

"What about the white van that I saw leaving the airport?"

"That belonged to Air France."

"Air France?"

"So, you see, Mister Sherman. We have nothing to go on."

"I see." Grant felt a helpless sense of disbelief. *This can't be happening.*

"Why don't you just go home and forget the whole thing. You are going to get a bill for the damage to the cab and the gate, but if you pay it, there won't be any further problems."

"Thank you, uh… What did you say your name was?"

"Wiseman, Kirk Wiseman," the agent gave a smile filled with pity for a former agent losing touch with reality.

"Thank you, Kirk. I'm sorry to bother you."

"You are free to go, if you go right home."

"I have to get a cab back to Manhattan to get my car."

"I'll call you a cab."

* * * * *

Mark O'Shay had no idea where he was. After regaining consciousness, he found himself in what appeared to be the back room of an office. There were no windows in the room, just a desk, two chairs, and a bookshelf. The dark haired man in the green t-shirt had given Mark back his cell phone and instructed him to call his secretary and tell her that he was taking off work the rest of the week. Green t-shirt held a gun on him the entire time.

Mark had a painful lump on the back of his head. Seeing the man in the green t-shirt walk by in the hall, Mark called out.

"Hey, you, in the green t-shirt…"

"You must be quiet," green t-shirt said in a foreign accent.

"Why am I here?"

"Our attempt to use the seminarian as a patsy didn't succeed."

"His name was David Owens if you care," Mark said.

"The detective you hired has caused us trouble. He was the one who first suspected that the seminarian did not commit suicide. We have been listening to his phone calls. He knows about us, and so do you."

"So I know about the guardians, why did you kidnap me?

"We have been watching your detective friend for days. After speaking to you on the phone, he drove into the city, and we followed him. As we expected, he was waiting for you at your apartment. We couldn't take the chance of letting you speak to him."

"I didn't say anything about the guardians."

"We were not sure if you had been told about our involvement in the death of the seminarian," green t-shirt said.

"Told by whom? The archbishop? I don't even know who you are!"

"And you probably never will."

"What do you mean?" Mark asked apprehensively.

"I want to show you something." The man in the green t-shirt handed a large manila envelope to Mark, who pulled out several photographs. His blood ran cold.

"These are my parents!"

"Yes, in Palm Beach, Florida. The view through that camera lens could just as easily be the view through the scope of a rifle with a silencer."

"You wouldn't!" Mark said, but even as he said it, he knew that they would.

"We have to ensure your silence. You must stop the detective from digging into the affairs of Father Quinn."

"Why did the guardians order the death of Father Quinn anyway?" Mark asked. "Because he fathered a child, or because he stole from the church?"

"Mister O'Shay, please, you should know the guardians do not concern themselves with the sexual antics of priests. That has gone on for centuries."

"Then why? The money?"

"The amount of money he misappropriated was pocket change. It was to keep him from exposing the list, of course."

"That's why I hired the detective. I'm trying to get the list!"

"The list must never become public!" the man in the t-shirt said, lowering his eyebrows for effect.

"How did you know to go after David Owens?" Mark asked.

"The boy at the seminary? We were told that he was an early suspect in the case."

"Who told you that? Who sent you?"

"You will be released tomorrow after you have had time to fully understand that you can never reveal anything about the guardians' involvement with Father Quinn."

"What about Grant Sherman? He's going to find me and ask me about the kidnapping. What am I supposed to tell him?"

"Tell him whatever you like, anything except the truth. You can leave tomorrow," green t-shirt said, taking the photographs of Mark's parents from his hands and returning them to the envelope, which he carried with him out of the room.

CHAPTER TWENTY-ONE

A week had gone by without Grant hearing anything from or about Mark O'Shay. He could have been dead for all Grant knew. The Fed Ex truck came to a slow stop with squeaking brakes at the curb outside Grant's office. Since the windows were open, Grant heard the truck come to a stop and glanced out the window. Besides the Fed Ex truck, he noticed an old Chevrolet Celebrity Eurosport with smoked windows. *That car was there yesterday, too.*

The Fed Ex deliveryman was a bulky but friendly giant of a young man, who didn't bother to knock, but walked right into the upstairs office.

"You Grant Sherman?"

"That's me! You ever play football?"

"All four years at Rutgers," the gentle giant replied with a smile.

"Too bad, we could have used you here at Princeton."

"No scholarships for athletes in the Ivy League." The young man said.

Yeah, but if you had gone to Princeton, you wouldn't be delivering packages for a living! "I guess you have a point," Grant said being diplomatic. Signing on the proper line, Grant looked at the shipping form inside the plastic cover on the outside of the cardboard envelope. The return address read, "Mr. Mark."

After the Fed Ex man had departed, Grant pulled the zip strip along the top of the envelope and removed one 3X5 index card. A handwritten message was written on it: "Grant, No tee time needed at Sawmill Golf Course on Mondays. Go there at 1 PM and play the first three holes. I will find you on the 4th hole by the lake." Grant looked at his watch – 10:30 AM. On the bottom of the card in large print was written, "They are watching you! Phone bugged and probably office too."

* * * * *

The first hole of Sawmill Golf Course is a par four, which is completely straight. Grant's first shot landed in the fairway about 250 yards from the tee. Playing alone, and his mind on meeting Mark O'Shay, Grant didn't care about his golf game. His fifth shot finally landed on the green twenty feet from the hole. Picking up the ball, Grant headed to the second hole, a short par three. Grant failed to reach the green on his first two shots. *How can I play golf under these circumstances?*

After playing the third hole, Grant was scanning the trees for Mark, but there was no sign of him. Standing on the tee box, he could see the lake on the left of the fairway about 100 yards away. *He said by the lake.* Teeing up a ball, Grant took a five iron and sent the ball directly into the water. Walking to the lake, Grant pretended to look for the ball, walking along the shore for fifty or so feet. Seeing nothing, he turned and walked toward the woods.

Stepping from behind a large evergreen tree, Mark O'Shay spoke Grant's name. With his back to Mark, Grant was startled and dropped his golf bag.

"Shit! Don't sneak up on me like that!" he said to Mark.

"Were you followed?"

"I think they were behind me until they saw that I was coming to the golf course. How about you?"

"I gave them the slip about two hours ago. I drove around all four leaves of a cloverleaf, drove 90 miles per hour for three minutes, and did a U-turn through the grass median. When I knew they were lost, I came here and waited for you."

"So you think they are tapping my phone?" Grant asked.

"I know they are, because they told me they were. They were also following you the afternoon they kidnapped me. They wanted to make sure I didn't tell you about them."

"We are talking about the guardians, right? The Priory of Sion?"

"Yes."

"So they are real?"

"They are real enough to have Father Quinn and David Owens killed." Mark said.

"I know they killed David Owens to make it look like he was the one that killed Father Quinn, but why did they kill Father Quinn? It doesn't make sense to me."

"I have to be careful, Grant. They are watching my parents and threatened to kill them if I didn't get you to back off the case and forget it."

"Forget it? And just let them get away with two murders? Are you kidding? The Suffolk County Police will never figure this out on their own."

"So you think they will listen to you?" Mark asked. "I heard your own Bureau buddies think you're nuts."

"I was trying to save your ass, Mark!"

"I didn't say you weren't, but you have to admit we don't have many allies in this deal."

"So, we'll just have to figure it out on our own and hand it to the police on a silver platter. I have a theory about what happened."

"I can't wait to hear it," Mark said sarcastically.

"I think the guardians were after Father Quinn before I was even hired. When Quinn was first attacked for the blood sample, the guardians wanted to know who had done it. They waited for me to dig up a suspect, intending all along to kill Father Quinn and place the blame on the suspect I found."

"Sounds good, but first of all, it doesn't tell us why they wanted him dead, and second, I hired you to find out what happened to Father Quinn."

"Was it your idea to hire an investigator in the first place?" Grant asked.

"Well, the archbishop asked me to find someone, but that was completely normal based on the circumstances – a priest had been attacked."

"I wonder," Grant said rubbing his chin. "Well, no matter what, we have to find out the motive for the guardians wanting Father Quinn out of the way."

"That's why I have his computer in the car," Mark said.

"You have Quinn's computer from the seminary?"

"Yes, just the tower, but we can hook up a different keyboard, mouse, and monitor."

"Great! We can call up his e-mail to see what Quinn was doing that was so distressing to the guardians!"

"They'll be waiting for you at your office, how about we take it to a neutral location?" Mark suggested.

"Like where?"

* * * * *

Sister Therese La Sue's computer lab on the second floor of Notre Dame High School in Easton, Pennsylvania was empty when Mark and Grant carried Father Quinn's HP Pavilion computer to one of the consoles. Mark was under the desk making the necessary connections when Sister La Sue walked in on what appeared to be a burglary in progress.

"One false move and I'll pull the fire alarm!" the elderly nun said loudly. Mark jumped and hit his head on the underside of the computer console.

"Hello, Sister Therese, It's just us, Grant Sherman and Mark O'Shay," Grant said.

"Hello, Sister!" Mark said, rubbing the top of his head. "We are on very important work for the Archdiocese of New York."

"Well, boys, nice of you to drop in to see me, but you could have asked for help or at least permission to use my computers. Besides, you are hooking that keyboard into the wrong plug."

"I am? Isn't this one for the mouse?" Mark asked.

"No," the nun said smiling. "The mouse goes in the purple plug on an HP Pavilion. The keyboard goes in the green one. What are you looking for if I may ask?"

"We need to read the e-mails from this computer. They might give us the motive for a crime," Mark O'Shay said trying not to tell the nun too much.

"So, it's a murder is it?" The nun said.

"I didn't say anything about a murder," Mark said.

"I've watched *Murder, She Wrote* enough to know that it's murder where you must find the motive. There!" Sister Therese said. "It's all connected. Fire it up." Grant turned on the power and the system booted itself up.

When he was offered the Windows screen, Mark selected the program called Outlook Express©, which would bring up Father Quinn's e-mail account.

"Everyone at the seminary used Outlook Express© just like we do at the archdiocese," Mark said.

"So, this is Father Quinn's computer!" Sister Therese said as more of a statement than a question, leaving her mouth open. Everyone in the clergy had been talking about the strange case of Father Paul Quinn's demise. Mark and Grant didn't answer.

Mark typed in Father Quinn's e-mail address and tried several passwords, but none worked.

"What else do you remember about Quinn's office?" Mark asked.

"There was the statue of St. Joseph, that he got beaned with," Grant said. "And there was a plastic M&Ms© figure."

"Plain or peanut?"

"What?"

"Was it the little round, red, plain M&M, or the larger, yellow, peanut M&M?"

"Yellow."

Mark tried "Peanut" and "Yellow" and "M&Ms" without success.

"What else?" Mark asked.

"Bingo!" Grant shouted.

"What?"

"That!" Grant said.

"What?

"The password!"

"So what is it?" Mark asked.

"Bingo, you piss worm!"

"Ohh!" Mark typed the word bingo and pressed enter. The e-mail account of Father Quinn appeared. "Shit! Oh, sorry, Sister."

"I've heard it before," she said.

"What's wrong?" Grant asked Mark.

"The inbox is empty. Everything has been deleted."

"Not completely," Sister Therese said. "There is still an electronic image in this machine, you just have to know how to call it back from deleted status. Until the exact memory byte is written on again, the old memory is still there. If the mail was recently deleted, the computer has probably not been used enough to overwrite the deleted e-mails, so they are probably still in the memory bytes. When you press the delete key, the memory bytes holding a certain document are slated for reuse, but until they are actually overwritten, the information remains there."

"So how do we bring back the right bytes that have what we want? How do we recall the right file and make it readable again?" Mark asked.

"Watch and learn, boys!" Sister Therese said, sitting down at the keyboard like she was about to play a piano concert.

"Are you a hacker, Sister?" Mark asked.

"The lord works in mysterious ways!" She answered.

Sister Therese typed, "DBXtract.exe" and pressed enter. A window opened with check boxes requesting a path. Sister typed, "WIN98\Application Data\Microsoft\Outlook Express" followed by "Inbox.dbx" in the file box. Then Sister Therese hit the "Extract" button.

Suddenly, e-mails appeared in Father Quinn's Outlook Express "sent" box. All the information held on the bytes destined for recycle was moved back onto readable Outlook mail folders and renamed, thus they appeared like new mail.

There were several e-mails to jw@tochos.org, which Mark double clicked and brought to the screen. It read:

> "There are numerous priests who not only subscribe to the ideas and beliefs promoted by this so called Priory of Sion, but they are even members of it. This heresy promoted by the Priory of Sion is against the very nature of Christianity. Without a resurrected Christ, the religion is nothing but the teachings of a man named Jesus. The Catholic Church cannot accept this retreat from the moral high ground. All members of this Priory of Sion among the clergy of the Roman Catholic Church must be purged. I have sent an official letter of inquiry to the Holy Father in Rome." It was signed only with a Q, which probably stood for Quinn.

"Well," Grant said. "There's your motive. Father Quinn was stirring the pot up for the Priory. They wanted to pull the thorn out of their side and silence Father Quinn for good."

"Hey," Mark said, "What's this?" Mark had clicked on the next e-mail, but it was not like any other he had seen. It read:

AR OR LR AM EM OM IO
TR LO AM AM OR YM
OO MO IM MM OR AE LR
YR OR TO LR MO MR
EM AM OR

OO TM TR OO EM TO ER

R Y T O

AR AM EM TM AM YM

EO MO IM AR MO MR

MO AE OM OR AR MO

MM AM MO TO OM EO

AE MO TR EM TO OR AM YM

TO TM YR

AR AM EM MO AE LR

TO MO YR

ER MR MO TO LR EM LR YM

LO AE OR

EO OR LM MO

IM EM AE LR

AR AM EM MO AE LR AE

AE LO AE AR MO OM LR MO MR

AP AM EM TM AM YM

TR MO TR OO MO AM AE

OR LR LR OR OM EO MO MR

AR.

TR LO AM AM OR YM

EM AE

IR TM EO TO

The message was signed again with only a Q.

"What do you make of it?" Mark asked.

"It's a code," Grant answered.

"No kidding! I meant what did you think the code might be?" Mark said shaking his head.

"In many codes using letters, the letters are substituted for numbers, which in turn are changed back into other letters to form words. The first thing we need to do is determine how many different letters are used in the code. It should be either 9 or 10." Mark began the process of counting.

"There are nine," Mark said finally.

"Okay, you will probably find that one letter is never used as the first letter in any pair of letters."

"It is R. R is never the first letter in any pair."

"Then R is the first letter of a nine-letter word or phrase that has no repeating letters."

"I'm losing you," Mark said. "How do you know this stuff?"

"I used to work for the FBI, remember? You have to unscramble the nine-letter word to make a key. R is the first letter in the word, so R is 'one'. The second letter will be 'two' and so on. The second, third, and fourth letters will also appear as a second letter in a group, there will only be four letters that are used as the second letter of a group."

"Really? Do you really understand this?" Mark asked. He was quite lost as to where Grant was going with this code stuff.

"Criminals use codes quite often, especially organized criminals and bookies."

"Okay, there is the R, an M, O, and an E. Those are the four letters that are used as the second letter of a pair," Mark said.

"So, R, M, O, & E are the first four letters of the jumbled word."

"ROME," Sister Therese said. "What are the other five letters?"

"L, I, T, A, and Y," Mark said.

"It's Italy! Rome, Italy! So we write it out like this..." Grant said as he wrote:

R	O	M	E	I	T	A	L	Y
1	2	3	4	5	6	7	8	9

"Did you ever look at the letters on a telephone dial?" Grant asked. "There are never any letters on the 1 key or the zero key – only the two through nine keys have letters. The first pair of letters in the code is AR. The letter A is the seventh letter in the key phrase ROME ITALY, so it refers to the 7 button on a phone dial. The second letter, R, is the first letter in the key phrase ROME ITALY, so it refers to the first letter on the seven button of the phone dial. The seven button has four letters, P Q R and S. That means that in the coded message, AR is the letter P." Grant was pleased with himself.

Mark was less impressed with Grant's code breaking skills than with the amount of work that was going to be needed to decipher the rest of the message.

"Do you know how long this is going to take us?" Mark asked.

"I'll go get you boys a pizza and some sodas," Sister Therese said.

"That will be great," Grant said, working steadily to decode the rest of Father Quinn's message.

"Beer would be better," Mark whispered.

After half an hour, Sister Therese returned with pizza and Pepsi.

"How are you coming along?" she asked.

"Just listen to this!" Grant read her the completed message.

"Patrick Murray – Belfast – wanted – IRA bombing 1960. Priory helped escape – French seminary. Now priest – new identity – USA. Have list – priests suspected Priory members attached. P. Murray is John."

"So Father Quinn had a list of Catholic priests who were suspected members of the Priory of Sion, and he was tracking a wanted fugitive from the IRA, who became a priest in France with the help of the Priory," Mark said.

"It's more than that," Grant said. "The last part of the code said that P. Murray is John. That means that he is the head of the Priory. Patrick Murray, an IRA terrorist and fugitive, is now a priest in the United States and is the leader of the Priory."

"Where is the attachment to the e-mail, the list?" Mark asked.

"It's not attached. It's been removed," Grant said.

"So what do we do?" Mark asked.

"We? We do nothing," Grant said. "I have a few ideas of where that list might be. But we can't be seen together. You said yourself that your parents are in danger." Grant turned to Sister Therese. "I know I can count on your discretion on this matter, Sister."

"Cross my heart and for the love of Jesus!" she said. "I won't tell a soul. You better be careful, Grant Sherman."

"I will, Sister." He felt like he was back in high school.

CHAPTER TWENTY-TWO

The e-mail address jw@tochos.org had caught Grant's eye the second he had seen it on the e-mail screen. What else could TOCHOS be except The Orphaned Children's Home of Salem, where Father Quinn had been sending all his money? It was time to do a little due diligence work on The Orphaned Children's Home of Salem.

Entering the name and address of the entity, Grant was informed by one database that TOCHOS was wholly owned by Wheels Up Limited on the island of Nevis. Several hours of further checking found a possible connection between Wheels Up Limited and a company called Imagdalation LTD on Cyprus. Grant had a contact on Cyprus, who could get incorporation records there. After a five minute phone conversation, catching up on things, the contact promised Grant a return call within a week. Grant agreed to pay the requested $800 for the search, but he already had a good idea who was going to be the owner of Imagdalation LTD on Cyprus, which owned Wheels Up Limited on Nevus, which owned TOCHOS, which was incorporated in Delaware, but doing business supposedly in Massachusetts.

The return call from Cyprus came on a Thursday afternoon, while Grant was away from the office. The message left on the voice mail was quick and to the point. "Imagdalation LTD – Cyprus is wholly owned by Simple Things Gallery, Incorporated in Massachusetts, which is wholly owned by Jo Wheeler.

Of course! jw@tochos.org is Jo Wheeler @ The Orphaned Children's Home Of Salem. She was pretty slick! How could I be so taken in by that woman? I never saw it coming with her naive act – as if she didn't know that Father Quinn was stealing the bingo money. She was playing like she was some small-time conspirator, while all along she was probably a full partner with Father Quinn. Jo Wheeler must have been the administrative assistant to Quinn in his quest to uncover the names of all the priests who are members of the Priory of Sion! And I missed it completely. I must be losing my touch. She probably has the attachment to Father Quinn's e-mail with the names of the priests who are members of the Priory, too.

With the arrival of morning, the situation called for a drive up to Boston for another interview with Jo Wheeler. Not wanting to go alone, Grant had called Michael Dennis on a pay phone and arranged to pick him up in Brooklyn on the way to Boston. Michael seemed to know as much or more about the Priory of Sion as anyone and was eager to help. Grant had flatly refused to let Mark O'Shay take part in any further investigation of the Priory. Grant had no relatives or loved ones for the Priory to threaten. He would continue to investigate, but he would make sure not to use his office phone. The Priory would have to have a damn good surveillance team to follow him, now that he knew they were out there.

It was ten in the morning when Grant pulled up in front of Joseph Komkovsky's apartment and picked up Michael, who was waiting outside by the curb.

"Good morning, Mister Sherman," Michael said.

"Please, call me Grant."

"Okay, so who is this woman we are going to see in Boston?" Michael asked.

"It's a long story, Michael."

"Well, it's a five hour drive to Boston. We should have enough time for the story and a few philosophical discussions."

After filling Michael in on his prior contacts with Jo Wheeler, the bingo scam, and The Orphaned Children's Home of Salem, Grant relayed his most recent findings about Jo Wheeler's string of offshore corporations and the coded e-mail from Father Quinn.

"So you think the guardians silenced Father Quinn because he wrote to Rome about them?" Michael asked.

"It seems like the most likely reason, don't you think?"

"Yeah, I guess so."

"The leader of the guardians, this John guy, what is his plan? Is he trying to be the Anti-Christ or something?" Grant asked.

"No, Mister Sherman, the Anti-Christ or the beast in Revelation was a political reference to Caesar Nero. The job of the leader of the guardians is to protect his members from exposure as heretics. Many of the members of the Priory of Sion are priests."

"That's another thing I don't understand," Grant said. "Why would a Catholic priest be a member of the Priory of Sion? Members of the Priory don't believe Jesus rose from the dead, which is a pretty large deviation from the Catholic faith."

"The guardians are Christians," Michael explained, "who believe that Jesus was just a man, like you and me. They share his vision of what man's relationship to God should be, as well as how to deal with their fellow man."

"They killed Father Quinn and David Owens. I wouldn't call that Christian," Grant answered.

"Like all fanatical religious sects, the guardians will kill for their cause. They see themselves as being persecuted by the rest of the church. They were forced to go underground, and they will kill to protect the identities of their members."

"What do you know about their leader, this guy who used to be Patrick Murray, the IRA bomber?" Grant asked as he made the turn onto Interstate 95 North toward Boston.

"Nothing. Is that who Father Quinn believed was John?"

"Yes, I have a friend in Toronto with the RCMP, who…"

"RCMP?" Michael repeated with a puzzled look.

"The Mounties. My buddy works for the Mounties in Toronto. I asked him to get an old photo of Patrick Murray from Interpol. He said they could do a little computer aging on it, too. I figure that will be the best way to find out who he is now."

"He could have had plastic surgery," Michael suggested.

"True, but it is worth a shot," Grant said. "Now what was that you said about Caesar Nero being the beast in Revelation?"

"In Revelation 13:15, it talks about the killing of those who would not worship the image of the beast. There were laws in ancient Rome that everyone had to worship Caesar as a god. The Christians refused, and were put to death by the thousands, particularly under Caesar Nero. Revelation specifically mentions that many who would not worship the image of the beast would be put to death. Revelation 13:18 says, "Here is wisdom. Let him who has understanding calculate the number of the beast, for it is the number of a man: His number is 666."

"Okay, what does that mean?" Grant asked.

"It is referring to the practice of Hebrew numerology, where every letter was given a numeric value. If you added up the numeric value of all the letters of a person's name, you got his number."

"Sounds simple enough," Grant said.

"In ancient Hebrew, Caesar Nero was actually called Kaisar Neron. In Hebrew, it was spelled Qh'sair N'ron. The 'Q' was worth 100, the 'h' was worth 5, the 's' was worth 60, the 'a' was worth 1, the 'r' was worth 200, the 'n' was worth 50, the 'r' was once again worth 200, and another 50 for the last 'n'. The total is 666 – Nero was the beast. There is no mystic prediction of the end of the world in Revelation." Michael had written the numbers out as he spoke, totaled them, and handed the paper to Grant. "The writer of Revelation, who is believed to be the same John who wrote the fourth Gospel, was trying to spread the idea that the end of the world, as the Jews knew it, was near. He was preparing them for the revolt against Rome."

"But the Romans kicked their ass!" Grant said.

"Yes, the nation of Israel was wiped off the map."

"So it really was the End of Days for Israel."

"But only the beginning for the guardians. To the guardians, the Roman victory was a hollow one, because Jesus and his wife and children were still alive. Eventually, Jesus conquered Rome by religious conversion. Rome became the center of Christianity."

"Pretty ironic," Grant admitted. "You really know your religious history."

"Actually, the more you know, the harder it is to believe. Answers breed more questions, and the Bible is full of questionable things."

By the time they reached Connecticut, they had discussed several theological questions including whether Adam and Eve had navels as depicted in the art of Michelangelo and the theory of transubstantiation. In Rhode Island, Michael began telling Grant about how he felt growing up without a father. Grant, who had a jerk for a father, thought he would have preferred Michael's childhood to his own.

"I guess you realized pretty early that you were different, because you didn't have a dad. With me, I didn't realize until much later in life that my father was a drunk with a mental illness. We lived through hell every day. Growing up crazy doesn't seem that difficult when you're a kid. You don't realize that you are using up all your patience."

"What do you mean?" Michael asked.

"I think that a person can only absorb a certain amount of stress in a lifetime. Once a person reaches that amount, they no longer function well under stress. The abuse and embarrassment that I endured seeped into me like a toxin and started rotting me from the inside. I can no longer deal with incompetent or rude people. Since I'm not afraid to stand up for myself anymore, I do it all the time now. If someone needs to be told off, I'm your man. If I think someone is an asshole, I tell him. I say what everyone else is only thinking. It's probably because I never got a chance to tell off my father."

"It's anger, because you have never forgiven your father," Michael said, sounding very priest-like.

"It not only affects your attitude," Grant said, ignoring Michael's observation, "It affects your health, too. You get stomach and intestinal problems, but the doctor can't find the cause. Your back hurts like hell all the time, but the MRI and X-rays are all negative. It's not post-traumatic stress disorder, because I don't have flashbacks. It's more than depression…"

"It's anger," Michael said again. "You have to let it go, or it will eat you alive."

"I have let it go, but I am in a constant fight to keep it from coming back." Grant looked over at his young traveling companion and realized that he had just said way too much about himself to a person he hardly knew. "So," he said, changing the subject, "did Father Quinn ever speak to you about the Priory of Sion?"

"No, I only know about them from my grandmother and some research I have done on my own."

* * * * *

It was late afternoon when Grant pulled the Cruiser into the parking lot across from Jo Wheeler's gallery in Salem. He and Michael got out and stretched their legs before crossing the street.

"Let me do most of the talking," Grant said. "You can speak, but let me ask some questions first to get the dialog going in the right direction."

"No problem," Michael smiled.

Jo Wheeler was opening boxes in the back room of the small gallery, while an older lady was standing behind the counter. Grant walked directly to the back of the gallery with Michael two steps behind. Jo looked up and recognized Grant right away.

"Well, you're back!" she said.

"It's Grant, Grant Sherman," he said in case she didn't remember.

"I know your name, silly. Mom, this is the detective from New York I told you about."

"Oh!" said the lady behind the counter with disinterest.

"What can I do for you, Grant?"

"This is Michael Dennis, Father Quinn's son," Grant said watching for the impact."

"His son?" Jo repeated looking at Michael and then back to Grant.

"Yes, we're here to ask you about The Orphaned Children's Home of Salem, which is owned by a shell company in Nevis, which is owned by another company in Cyprus, which is owned by Simple Things Gallery, Incorporated, which is owned by you, Jo."

"Wow! I underestimated you, Grant," Jo said. If she was rattled, her confident smile didn't give it away."

"I think we underestimated each other, Jo. You had that story of the Amy Anderson payment and the fake lawsuit all ready for someone like me to come in asking about The Orphaned Children's Home of Salem. I asked about the bingo money and your little misdirection took my attention right away from the real secret – The Orphaned Children's Home of Salem doesn't exist. Father Quinn wasn't donating his stolen bingo money to some charity. He was funding your underground intelligence gathering organization."

"That's right," Jo admitted.

"So, all I want to know is how much do you know about what Father Quinn was doing?" Grant said.

"What do you mean?" Jo asked.

"He knows about the Priory of Sion," Michael said. "He knows that Father Quinn was trying to expose the priests who are members of the Priory. He knows that Father Quinn wrote to Rome about them. He knows that's why Father Quinn was killed."

"We are here to finish the job that Father Quinn started," Grant added.

"I see," Jo said after a short pause. She was deciding whether or not to trust them. The fact that he was working with Father Quinn's son, Michael, did more to convince her to trust Grant than anything else.

"What do you say, Jo?" Grant asked.

"Mom, will you close up the store for me?"

"Where are you going?" her mother asked in an annoyed voice. She didn't like detectives.

"I have to talk to Grant and Michael about some companies of mine."

"Okay, whatever."

"Let's go get some coffee," Jo suggested.

* * * * *

Over steaming mugs of cafe latte, Jo took Grant and Michael into her confidence. She told them she had been terribly upset by the death of Father Quinn, but not surprised by it. Father Quinn had been determined to write to Rome about the Priory of Sion's members inside the Catholic priesthood despite Jo's warnings of possible retaliation.

"He got their attention all right," Jo said.

"His coded e-mail mentioned someone named Patrick Murray, an IRA fugitive," Grant said to Jo.

"Yes, Murray became a priest in France and changed his name. Father Quinn was sure that this person was now the leader of the Priory."

"John," Michael added.

"That's right, all the leaders of the Priory of Sion change their name to John," Jo replied.

"I've asked a buddy in the Royal Canadian Mounted Police to get an Interpol photo of Patrick Murray from London. He thinks he can get some computer aging done on it to give us an idea of what the leader of the Priory of Sion looks like today."

"That will be great, Grant!" Jo answered. "What a good idea!"

"What else do you know about this John fellow, and the workings of the Priory?" Grant asked Jo.

"Well, Paul – I mean, Father Quinn and I hired a guy in Africa to check out some activity that was being conducted by the Priory there. He found some interesting things."

"Really?" Grant said with interest. "Like what?"

"Have you ever heard of the Kingdom of Aksum?" Jo asked them.

"No," Grant said.

"Yes," Michael answered. "Aksum is located in present day Ethiopia and was supposed to be the kingdom of one of King Solomon's sons, Menelik. Menelik was sent on a journey the full length of the Red Sea, to return his mother, the Queen of Sheba, to her homeland. Solomon was worried about the safety of his son and his mother on this dangerous voyage, so he supposedly sent a group of trusted noblemen along with the Ark of the Covenant to protect them."

"That's right! I'm impressed with your knowledge of Bible legends," Jo said.

"Why do you think I brought him along?" Grant asked.

"I see," Jo said. "The Ark of the Covenant is one of the most coveted relics in all of the Judeau-Christian world, along with the true cross and the Holy Grail, which some people think is the cup that Jesus used at the Last Supper– Even Hitler looked for these things!"

"Legend has it," Michael began with authority, "that the Holy Grail, or San Greal in Latin was really the Sang Real, which means Royal Blood – a reference to the holy bloodline of Jesus. The Priory believes that they have found the body of the son of Jesus in France, so they consider that they have already found the Sang Real or Holy Grail."

"Right again," Jo said.

"As far as the true cross goes," Michael continued, "The Templars claimed to have it at one time during the Crusades. If that was true, then the Priory probably still has it."

"That is what we have been told, also," Jo said.

"That leaves the Ark of the Covenant, which I guess the Priory would stop at nothing to obtain," Grant said with skepticism.

"That is what the activity in Africa was supposed to be all about. We paid a lot of money to get people with inside knowledge to help us. We know the Priory was looking for the Ark of the Covenant in Mekele, near the Simen Mountains, about 300 miles north of Addis Ababa in Ethiopia, the site of the ancient capital city of Aksum."

"You're serious?" Grant found himself asking. *This is so incredible that it's almost funny!* "Where's Harrison Ford?" He snickered at his own joke.

"I'm not kidding about this!" Jo said. "These guys are like a cult. They take these artifacts very seriously!"

"But the Ark of the Covenant?" Grant protested. "You don't actually believe the Hebrews sent their most prized possession to Ethi-freaking-opia, do you?"

"What I believe is not important, Grant," Jo said solemnly. "What the Priory of Sion believed and did is all that we were interested in."

"So, what did you find out?" Michael asked excitedly.

"Our man reported to us that the expedition went from Mekele to the shore of Lake Tana, the source of the Blue Nile River," Jo continued.

"Blue Nile?" Grant asked.

"As opposed to the White Nile," Jo informed him, "which begins at Lake Victoria in Uganda, and then runs north into Sudan. The Blue Nile begins at Lake Tana in Ethiopia then also flows north into Sudan. The Blue Nile and the White Nile run together to form the Nile River at the city of Khartoum."

"Are you sure you're not a geography teacher?" Michael joked.

"I've been studying the area recently."

"So what happened to this expedition the Priory sent to Ethiopia?" Grant asked.

"After a week or so at Lake Tana, they chartered a plane to Nairobi, Kenya, where they placed a crate on a Kenyan Airways flight to Mahe' in the Seychelles, which are a group of 115 islands about 1000 miles east of Nairobi in the Indian Ocean."

"That's an offshore haven for money laundering and shell companies and all," Grant said.

"Yes, that's why we think the Priory went there. They probably have bank accounts and companies there," Jo said. "Which is why I'm going there."

"WHAT?" Grant screamed. "You're just going out into the middle of the Indian Ocean by yourself? These weirdoes at the Priory won't think twice about putting a bullet in you!"

"I won't be by myself. I'm supposed to meet a source there, and I was thinking of asking you to go with me for protection," she said, giving him a confident smile.

"I liked it better when I thought you were just a ditzy blonde who ran a gallery," Grant said.

"Well, I wish I could make the trip with you two," Michael said, "but Archbishop Moreau has reinstated me at Immaculate Conception Seminary. I have to go to class and study for finals."

"Good for you," Grant said.

"So, do we have a date?" Jo asked Grant. He wondered how he could have ever been fooled into thinking that Jo was just some church lady that got duped into playing free bingo cards by a crooked priest. *Blonde hair and a chest like Barbie© will fool a guy every time.*

"I suggest we fly from Newark," Grant said. "Kenya Airways is a partner of KLM and Northwest Airlines. Northwest has a daily flight from Newark to Amsterdam, where we can catch KLM to Nairobi, and Kenya Airways to Mahe' – We can book it all at once. First class I assume?"

"Of course, money is not a problem," Jo smiled. "I'll book the flights and call you with the flight times. We can meet in Newark Airport."

"It's a done deal, then," Grant said. "I'll look forward to hearing from you – No, wait! I'll call you! Don't call my office, okay?"

"Okay, I'll wait for your call tomorrow night."

CHAPTER TWENTY-THREE

The trip to Africa was scheduled to depart from Newark, New Jersey on Monday at 5 PM. Jo was there at the gate to meet him at 3:30, just as they had agreed. The eight-hour flight to Amsterdam would have them landing at midnight New York time, which would be 6 AM Tuesday in Amsterdam. After a four-hour layover, they would take another eight-hour flight to Nairobi, landing at 7 PM local time, too late to make the Tuesday connection to the Seychelles. A night at the Nairobi Hilton would be required before catching the Wednesday morning flight on Kenya Airways to Mahe' International Airport. It would be physically exhausting, but Grant was looking forward to the adventure. There were worse things to do than fly off to exotic places with an attractive blonde.

"What does your husband think of you flying off to Africa with a strange man?" Grant asked.

"You're not <u>that</u> strange," she joked. "Besides, I've been divorced for two years."

"Oh?"

"Down boy," she said with a smile. Grant laughed and changed the subject.

"What do you know about this source we're going to meet?"

"He's been selling information to Paul Quinn for years. We have no reason to think he isn't on our side."

"Well, just so you know, I mailed a letter to Michael Dennis that contained the computer aged Interpol photo of Patrick Murray, the supposed leader of the Priory. If anything happens to us, he'll take it to the proper authorities."

"Do you have a copy of the photo with you?" Jo asked with interest.

"Sure, here." Grant produced a 5 x 7 enlargement of a very old, arrest photo of Patrick Murray. The hair had been thinned and made gray, and the wrinkles were obviously computer generated. However, it did help one imagine how the elderly Patrick Murray might appear today.

"I don't recognize him," Jo said.

"Did you think you would?"

"I don't know, but I bet Paul Quinn would have known him."

"Why didn't he get the police involved earlier?" Grant asked.

"Paul didn't trust the police. He only trusted me."

"Well, it's too late for him to identify the photo. Who else do you think might recognize the man in the photo?"

"We could only take it to someone in the church that we were sure that we could trust," Jo said.

"Any ideas?"

"What about the person that hired you in the first place?"

"That was Mark O'Shay. He works for the Archbishop in New York, so I guess it was his archbishop who hired me."

"Maybe that is the best place to go," Jo suggested.

"They threatened to kill Mark's parents, and they kidnapped him for a while to make the point. I don't want to ask him to do anything else. If I did, and something happened to his parents because of it, I wouldn't be able to live with myself. What about the list of priests on Father Quinn's list of Members of the Priory of Sion?"

"What about it?" Jo asked.

"We could use it to make sure that we didn't go to anyone at the Catholic Church who is a member of the Priory."

"Do you have it with you?" Jo asked.

"No, I thought Father Quinn sent it to you. The attachment had been removed from the e-mail we recovered from his computer."

"It must be still in my e-mail files – I never opened the document. I just saw the attachment."

"Weren't you curious about who was on the list?" Grant asked.

"I wouldn't have known any of them anyway. Paul just sent it to me as a back up. I'm sure he sent it to Rome with his official letter!"

"What if someone intercepted that letter? There sure hasn't been any reaction to it that I've seen. We'll get the list of priests from your computer together as soon as we get back home."

"Okay. What are we going to do with it?"

"That's a good question, I don't know anyone with the church, and most of the FBI agents and police in New York think I'm crazy. We'll find someone. Didn't Father Quinn have any other priests that he was working with on this?"

"Not that he told me about. He told me that he and I were the only ones who knew about this. Then he said he had sent it to Rome."

"And then he died! I bet that letter never got through." Grant would have been more comfortable going back to Jo's right then and getting the list of Priory members from her computer. *There has to be someone in the Bureau that will listen to me. Maybe if I took Mark O'Shay with me. They could give him protection for his parents. I wonder if they would listen to me?*

* * * * *

Grant was able to sleep some of the way to Amsterdam, which ruined his ability to sleep for the rest of the night. Since Jo was sleeping on the flight from Amsterdam to Nairobi, there was no conversation to help pass the time. He finally resorted to several cocktails to slow his thoughts, which were constantly churning in his brain. He just wanted to get off this glorified waiting room.

The plane landed hard at JKI Airport in Nairobi, shaking both Grant and Jo awake. The European passengers all applauded the pilot's efforts.

"It looked like you slept well," Grant said to Jo, whose hair was a little mussed.

"I don't like people to see me when I just wake up."

"You can't have any fun that way," Grant teased.

"I've been known to make some exceptions. What time is it here?"

"Time to go to the hotel and eat dinner, almost 7 PM."

After waiting for half an hour for the luggage, Grant and Jo found the Hilton shuttle bus. The drive to the hotel was a twenty-minute education in the third world. Though it was getting dark, there was no hiding the poverty that lurked around every corner of the city. Flowered trees gave the illusion of a tropical paradise, but homeless men selling grilled corn on the cob were just as prevalent.

The restaurant at the Nairobi Hilton was like those in any American city, except for the Kenyan waiters dressed like British butlers and a buffet where most of the dishes had been prepared with curry. Grant opened the lid of a tray marked "rabbit," finding legs that looked suspiciously small for rabbits.

"I wonder if they mean rat bits instead of rabbit?" he joked, but he didn't serve himself any.

"Where's your sense of adventure?" Jo asked. "Curried rat never hurt anyone."

"That's okay," he said smiling. "I think I'll let the rats crawl on by." Grant closed the lid on the rabbit and found some fish. "Here we go – fish! You can't really screw up baked fish."

"Do you think it's safe to eat the lettuce?" Jo asked.

"I wouldn't, and don't drink anything with ice in it."

"I guess you're right."

"You guess? How many shots did you have to get to come here?" Grant asked, his own arms still sore.

"Six."

"I rest my case!" he said with a Groucho Marx delivery.

Jo looked at Grant's plate, which held baked fish, rice, and steamed cauliflower.

"Your whole plate is full of white stuff!" she laughed.

"So I'll order a Coke©! That's not white."

"You're a treasure!" she said. "One minute you're James Bond, and the next minute you're Hawkeye from *M*A*S*H.*"

"Even the Army didn't serve rats, just liver and fish. In fact, Hawkeye once said he had eaten a river of liver and an ocean of fish."

"See what I mean?"

Dinner was over quickly, as the food was nothing special. Since all of the shops in the hotel lobby were closed for the day, and it was not recommended that rich Americans walk around downtown Nairobi at night, there was nothing to do but go up to the rooms. Grant followed Jo to her room and suggested that they check to see what was on television, but other than three soccer games, German news, CNN and the Hallmark Channel, there was nothing to see. Grant had the room next door to Jo's, but there was no adjoining door.

"Do you think it is safe for me to stay in this room alone?" Jo asked.

"As long as you use the deadbolt and the safety latch thing." Grant didn't know what to call the sliding lock that had taken the place of the old chain locks. "And don't open the door for anyone except me – not room service, not housekeeping, not anyone!"

"I think I'd feel safer if you stayed in here, too."

Does she know what she just said? And if so, what the hell does she mean by that?

"Uh… I…"

"This king size bed is really two twin beds pushed together," she said. "If you want to be prudish, we can move them apart."

"We don't have to move them apart on my account," Grant said, wondering if that sounded more like James Bond or Hawkeye.

"It's not like I asked you to have sex with me, Grant."

"I know. No, it's fine. Whatever!" *James Bond never would have said, "Whatever!"*

The night was as unremarkable as the dinner had been.

* * * * *

Since their internal clocks had not adjusted to Africa time, Jo and Grant were up and ready to do something at 7 AM. Deciding to pass on a breakfast buffet of runny scrambled eggs and overcooked sausage links, Jo and Grant decided to check out the souvenir dealers. Nairobi is the gathering point for all tourists going on safaris to the Masai Mara game preserve or to see the endless sea of pink flamingos at Lake Nakuru a little farther north. The craft industry in Nairobi has exploded to make certain that no rich tourist goes home without several carved or beaded mementos of their adventure to the Dark Continent.

Jo was pleasantly surprised to find the souvenir shops in the hotel lobby were open already. Animals carved from deep blue lapis lazuli and green malachite were abundant. The wooden carvings were even more impressive, some done in ebony and others in a material known as stone wood. Not all carvings were art quality, some were only crudely carved animals obviously intended to be toys. Jo selected an ebony giraffe with a turned head and bent legs. Each muscle and eyelash could be seen, making it a true work of art.

"If he says he wants a hundred bucks, that means you can probably get it for forty," Grant informed Jo.

"You think he will ask that much?"

"That's a really nice one. It's worth every bit of forty," Grant said.

"How much?" Jo asked, holding up the giraffe.

"Shillings or dollars?" the clerk asked.

"Dollars."

"One hundred dollars," the clerk said.

"It's too much," Jo said, returning the giraffe to the shelf. However, the clerk was there in an instant and picked the piece up and handing it back to Jo.

"What's your best price? I give you a good deal."

"Forty," Jo offered.

"No, it's no good! Seventy," the clerk said.

"Forty!" Jo said firmly.

"Sixty."

"No!'

"Change your price," the clerk said, trying to teach Jo the proper etiquette of bargaining, but Jo was not playing along. She replaced the giraffe on the shelf and walked away. "Okay, okay, your price! Forty!" The clerk had the giraffe in one hand and the other extended for the money, which Jo placed in his palm.

"Can you wrap it for me?" she asked in slow English. She turned to Grant with a puzzled look. "How did you know what price he would take?"

"These vendors always try to get you to pay more than double the price. If you cut their price in half and knock off another ten percent, you're about right. The jewelry is the best deal, if you know what you're looking for. All the amber in Africa is fake, but the silver is priced pretty reasonably for the work put into it."

"What about the tribal bead work?" Jo asked, looking at some Masai wedding ornamentation.

"You have to remember that beads were only recently introduced to African culture by the Dutch. The real tribal ceremonial stuff are the wooden masks," Grant said taking a highly polished Ivory Coast elephant man mask from a hook on the wall. "The three sacred animals are the elephant, the crocodile, and the ibis. Ivory Coasters will almost always depict one of the three. They are by far the most sought after masks in Africa for the craftsmanship."

"How do you know this stuff?" Jo asked. "You've been here before, haven't you?"

"I've been a lot of places," Grant replied without answering.

"Where all have you been, Grant?"

"Africa – both East and West Africa, Greece, Israel, China, Russia, Ukraine, Estonia, Austria, the U.K., Costa Rica, Antigua, Mexico, Canada, Puerto Rico, hell the only continents I haven't been to are Australia and Antarctica, and not one of those trips was a vacation."

"All work and no play?"

"I sometimes manage some sightseeing and culture appreciation along with my investigation or consultation. I'm sorry to change the subject, but I think we should head for the airport and check in. This is Africa, we don't want to miss our flight and have to wait until Saturday."

"Sure, call us a cab, and I'll go up and get my suitcase."

"Okay. Meet me in the lobby in fifteen minutes."

* * * * *

There was food on the plane, and it was mercifully edible. The flight seemed short compared to their ordeal of the day before. Looking out the window on the right side of the plane, Grant could see the first of several granite outcroppings in the water. While the smaller ones were bare, the larger ones were green with lush tropical growth on top, but dark gray under the water. Some of the Seychelles are encircled with white sandy beaches, which turn the ocean from deep blue to light aqua. The Seychelles are really the top of a large mountain range, which was left stranded when the super-continent broke up millions of years ago sending India smashing into Asia, raising the Himalayas. Coral patches have begun to grow in the shallower water, forming atolls.

The landing at Mahe' Airport was interesting, as it was a completely open-air affair. The customs check was just a matter of making sure you found your bag and got it to a taxi.

Grant found an older taxi driver, who didn't appear to be a physical threat, and hired him to take them to the Allamanda Guest House on the southeast coastline. From there, they would be able to conduct their business in Victoria's town center. Victoria was a sleepy little town after sunset, but would be quite lively during the morning, once banking business started. There was even a thirty-foot tall miniature of Big Ben in the center of town, but the plastic, gas station pennant flags did make the place look a little cheesy.

The Allamanda Guest House was a white, two-story, ten-unit hotel surrounded by palm and almond trees near the beach. There were four units each on the eastern and western side of the building, and two units each on the north and south. Grant and Jo registered as husband and wife and took a unit that had a "mountain view."

"A mountain view it says," Grant complained, "like that's something good! A mountain view means you didn't get an ocean view. It shouldn't be promoted like it's something a person would want!"

"Okay, Jerry Seinfeld, you made your point." Jo exhaled and bit her tongue.

"Am I annoying you?" Grant asked.

"What ever gave you that idea? You should be an investigator!"

"Okay, okay! Where and when are we supposed to meet Mister X?" Grant rolled his eyes for maximum sarcasm. "Probably tonight at midnight in the graveyard, or some shit!"

"He is supposed to be at the church near the town square at 3 PM," Jo said.

"How will we know him?"

"He is going to ask us if the Yankees won last night."

"You're kidding! A password? This is like Don Adams on *Get Smart!*"

"When he asks us, we're supposed to say it was a rain out."

"And then he takes out his magic decoder ring?"

"Why are you being like this? I didn't make up the stupid passwords."

"This whole situation is not right somehow. I don't know what it is, but something is wrong. I don't understand this whole Ark of the Covenant expedition you are checking into. I thought you wanted to expose this group."

"I think it is important to know exactly what they are up to, so we can expose everything they are doing and who is doing it," Jo answered.

"Well, this reminds me of dogs chasing a lion."

"What's your point?" Jo asked.

"The dogs have a lovely time chasing until they actually corner the lion, who proceeds to slash them to bits one after the other. Sometimes the worst thing that can happen is to catch what you've been chasing." Grant was out of his element here and felt exposed. *This woman has no idea how easy it would be for someone to pop us both in the head and drop our bodies into the ocean for the sharks. We are in the middle of freaking nowhere!*

CHAPTER TWENTY-FOUR

At 3 o'clock, Jo and Grant entered the small church near the square in Victoria town center. They were almost late because Jo had to stop to get a view of Esmerelda, the world's oldest tortoise at 153 years old. The church was empty.

"It was just a stupid turtle!" Grant said.

"We didn't miss anything, he's not even here yet," Jo snapped back.

"Excuse me," came a voice from the front of the church. Grant noticed a short, thin African priest, who was about 50 years old, smiling at them.

"Oh, sorry, Father. We were just meeting someone here." Grant said dismissively.

"I see," replied the priest. "Would you happen to know whether the Yankees won last night?" Grant's eyes widened, and he looked at Jo expecting her to deliver the countersign. She froze.

"I forgot what I'm supposed to say!" she whispered to Grant.

"Rained out," Grant replied. "Nice to meet you," Grant said, offering his hand. The priest shook Grant's hand and smiled, but he said nothing. The priest had crooked teeth and obviously was not accustomed to the use of toothpaste or deodorant.

"I have your money," Jo said finally. She handed over an envelope thick enough to choke a moose.

"Jesus Christmas! How much have you been toting around with you? Shit, there are laws about crossing borders with thousands of dollars in you pockets!" Jo ignored him.

"The money is not for me," the priest finally said. "It is for the children. You are looking for the man who established the businesses and bank accounts for the religious archaeological expedition to Ethiopia," the African priest said.

"That's right," Jo nodded her head in agreement. "I got a message that said the Priory had chartered the trip to search for religious relics. You have the name of the man that does all their organizing here?"

"He is in the corner office of the white building by the clock in town center. You will see a maroon awning. His name is Swanson, Henry Swanson."

"Thank you," Jo said, turning to leave.

"Whoa! Wait a minute! How do you know that? Are you the one who gave Father Quinn the list of priests who are members of this organization?" Grant fired questions faster than the priest could answer them.

"I am a priest, and I am a member of this organization, as you call it. That is how I know what I know. Good day!" The priest bowed and walked back behind the altar of the church.

"I guess we go down the block and talk to Henry Swanson," Jo said.

Henry Swanson was a tall Black man with unusually white, perfect teeth. He spoke English with a British accent and carried at least 250 pounds on his six and a half foot frame. The diplomas on the walls of Swanson's office proclaimed that he had received an MBA from United Business Institute in Brussels, Belgium and a JD from Southern California University for Professional Studies. The office was small and shabby, but it was situated on the best corner in Victoria.

Grant looked around at the brochures and literature, which offered offshore companies in chains of four, each in a different tax haven to confound government investigators and confuse an audit trail. One could also buy a bank chartered, licensed, and ready to do business in the Seychelles. If you owned your own bank, you would be the person to decide what was suspicious activity and what wasn't. Grant took a few business cards.

"So, you sell any banks to anybody lately?" Grant asked to break the ice.

"We tend to respect privacy and secrecy more than small talk," Mr. Swanson answered.

"What can you tell us about a group called the Priory of Sion?" Grant asked again.

"I don't know what you are talking about." Swanson said.

"How about now?" Jo asked, pulling four one hundred dollar bills out of her pocket.

"You said the Priory of Sion? Let me think, no, they called themselves something else. I think you are talking about Lamb Management, a company here in the Seychelles."

"What does Lamb Management own?" Grant asked making a note of the company name on the back of one of Henry Swanson's business cards.

"I'm not allowed to tell about a client's personal information!" Swanson said, almost convincingly. After Jo pulled two more hundreds out of her pocket, Swanson continued. "I think you would be better served doing business with POS, Ltd., which is a BVI company with a bank account in Aruba!"

"Is that the platform? Grant asked, "in the BVI?"

"Noooo," Swanson said with baited breath, glancing at Jo again. She pulled two more hundreds from her pocket, for a total of $800 U.S.

"That's all there is, pal!" Jo said convincingly. "Where is the end of the daisy chain?"

"In Belize."

"Company?"

"Guardian Services, Limited, with a bank account at Banco de Costa Rica."

"Are you sure?" Grant asked.

"I set it up myself!" Swanson said as he scratched his oily head.

"Is there an actual office in Belize?" Grant asked.

"Yes, with a staff of one. He handles the bank transfers with the bank in Costa Rica – All in Spanish."

"What was all this stuff about an expedition into Ethiopia to find a religious object?" Jo asked.

"That was for your benefit!" said another voice in the room. The short African priest from the church walked into Swanson's office. "We knew Father Quinn's accomplice would come asking for information about how the expedition was organized," the priest said. "The sole purpose of the expedition was lure you here on a fact finding mission."

"So you're a double agent, and you set us up," Grant said to the priest.

"We wanted to know the name of the man who was helping Father Quinn track down the members of the Priory, but it turned out to be a woman." The priest motioned toward Jo. "Mister Swanson was assigned to find out who was helping Father Quinn in his quest to expose the Priory."

"What was your motive, Mrs. Wheeler, for helping Father Quinn raise money and organize his investigation?" Henry Swanson asked.

"At first he let me use some of the money to start my business," Jo said. "Then, once he trusted me, he asked me to help him with his work."

"You should have quit when Father Quinn died!" Swanson said producing a .380 caliber semi-automatic pistol. "And you, Mister Sherman, are proving to be much more trouble than you are worth. Now if you would kindly walk with us back outside to my Land Rover©." Swanson and the African priest followed closely behind them as they followed Swanson's directions.

"You promised there would be no violence!" the African priest said in a loud whisper to the much larger Swanson.

"You have done your duty and been nicely paid, Father. Now if you would be so kind, you can go back to church!"

"I don't want any blood on my hands!" the priest said not bothering to whisper.

"I said go!" Swanson yelled at the priest, who opened the back door on the passenger side of the Land Rover© for Jo and bowed. As he bowed, the priest's hand went to inside his cassock and produced a small revolver, which he quickly tossed onto the floorboard in front of Jo. Then he quickly walked away.

"You drive Mr. Sherman, so I can keep my eyes on you," Swanson said getting in the front passenger seat. Grant got behind the wheel and looked around at Jo. She gave a quick wink, but Grant didn't know what she had in mind. *I guess I'll just keep his attention focused on me.*

"Why did you give us the information about the Priory's offshore companies and bank accounts if you were going to kill us?"

"You paid me for the information. I can always use $800!" Swanson smiled.

"You'll never get away with this, Swanson! People know where we are, and who we came to see. I have already given papers to people for safekeeping. If I don't come home, they will go to the authorities." Grant spoke loudly trying to keep Swanson's attention focused on him.

“Drive west, out of town,” he said. Grant followed the instructions, driving along the bumpy road that headed out to the ocean. “I thought you would like to take a little boat ride,” Swanson said smugly. “Take that gravel road to the right.”

Grant turned onto the gravel road, which took them though a thick stand of palm trees. The quick transition from equatorial sun to deep shade made everything go dark until their eyes could adjust. The loud crack exploded in Grant’s ears, as Swanson’s blood and brains splattered onto the inside of the windshield. Grant brought the Rover to a rapid stop, his ears ringing, and looked at Jo. She had a stunned expression, which made it clear she hadn’t expected the amount of noise and gore that resulted when she pulled the trigger of the revolver.

“Where the hell did you get a gun?” Grant asked.

“The little priest slipped it to me. He didn’t want Swanson to kill us.”

“I don’t think he had this in mind either! We’ve got to get the hell out of here! I suggest we ditch the Rover and walk back to Victoria town center and take a cab right to the airport. We need to be on the next plane out of here!”

“Take the eight hundred dollars out of his pocket!” Jo said.

“Why? We have to – No, you’re right. It is better if this looks like a robbery. I’ll take his wallet, watch, and ring, too.”

“What about the hotel and the luggage?” Jo asked.

“They have an imprint of your credit card. Once we are out of here, we can call and have them send our luggage back to America.

They won't care as long as they get paid. You can say it was a medical emergency, and we had to fly out immediately. That isn't even a lie – If we don't get off this island, we may not live much longer!"

* * * * *

At the airport, which was only about five miles from Victoria town center, there was a line at the British Airways counter, so Grant and Jo got in line.

"I guess we are going to London," Grant said. "Let's go to the first class counter, so we won't have to wait here." Jo nodded and followed Grant to the vacant first class counter.

"May I help you?" said a cheerful young lady with Asian features.

"Yes, we want two first class tickets on the flight that is just about to leave," Grant said as Jo snapped her American Express card onto the counter. The young lady behind the ticket counter typed several strokes on her keyboard and smiled.

"We have plenty of space available, but only in business class, as there is no first class offered on this flight."

"Fine! Book it!" Grant said.

"Will you be checking any bags?"

"No."

"It will take just a few minutes to print the tickets. May I see your passports, please?"

Grant and Jo walked to the gate and were allowed to board right away. Grant, however, wasn't comfortable until the flight attendant closed the door and the airliner began to taxi toward the runway.

"We made it!" Jo said with a huge sigh.

CHAPTER TWENTY-FIVE

Back at the computer lab at Notre Dame High School in Easton, Pennsylvania, Sister Therese La Sue had been running a program designed to decipher computer passwords. She had concluded that the attachment on Father Quinn's coded e-mail was indeed attached to the e-mail, but was protected by a password. It would appear when the proper password was typed after clicking on the attachment. After seven hours of trying different combinations at three per second, the program stopped. With the word "Galatians" on the line, suddenly the screen was filled with names.

"I just hit the jackpot!" Sister Therese said, as she ran to the phone to call Mark O'Shay at the Archdiocese of New York. She waited as Mark's secretary transferred the call to his desk.

"Hello, this is Mark O'Shay."

"Mark, this is Sister Therese."

"Yes, Sister. Is everything okay?"

"Everything is fine, Mark, but I wanted to know if you would like to come out and see some things I bought back from Rome, Italy. You know we were talking about Rome, Italy before?"

"Oh yeah! Yes, I remember. You say you brought something back?"

"I sure did – a real treasure. You really need to come and see it."

"It will take at least two hours to get there," Mark said.

"I'll be right here where I met you last time," Sister Therese said, enjoying the cloak and dagger aspect of it all.

"I'm on my way."

* * * * *

Grant had promised to call Michael Dennis every day around noon New York time while he was in Africa. In the event that the call had not been made by 1 PM, Michael was to take the envelope with the computer-aged photo of Patrick Murray, the IRA terrorist turned priest and leader of the Priory of Sion, to the authorities, although no specific authorities were mentioned. Now that the day's phone call from Grant had not come, Michael wished that Grant had been a little more specific as to which authorities he was supposed to give the photo.

Michael recalled that the photo had been sent to Grant form the Royal Canadian Mounted Police, which meant they did not know the new identity of the person in the photo. Michael decided that the best thing to do would be to attempt to identify the man in the photo.

Inserting his thumb under one end of the flap on the back of the envelope, Michael carefully tore the envelope open and removed the photo of Patrick Murray.

"Oh my god!" Michael said to himself. The face looking back at him from the photo was quite familiar. "It can't be!" He decided to call the Toronto office of the Royal Canadian Mounted Police and give them the identity of long time IRA fugitive Patrick Murray. *They'll know what to do about it.*

* * * * *

Mark O'Shay drove over eighty miles an hour out Interstate 78 West across New Jersey toward Easton, Pennsylvania, which is located just on the other side of the Delaware River from Phillipsburg, New Jersey. He was sure that Sister Therese had uncovered the attachment from Father Quinn's e-mail – the list of priests who were members of the Priory of Sion that every member of the guardians sought.

Pulling into the parking lot in front of Notre Dame High School, the front tires of Mark's Saab protested against the blacktop with a high-pitched squeal. Slamming the transmission into park, he pulled the keys, but didn't bother to lock the doors. He ran for the front door of the school.

Entering the computer lab, Mark called out Sister Therese's name.

"Over here!" the nun said from a table on the side of the room where she had been printing. "I found the list. I'm printing out a bunch of copies."

"Who do you think we should sent it to?" Mark asked.

"Well, not to anyone on this list, that's for sure," Sister Therese said handing Mark a copy of the list. "Take a look at the top of the list."

"Oh, shit!"

"I thought that's what you would say," the nun chuckled.

* * * * *

Having located the complete address and phone number of the RCMP in Toronto, Michael had written a letter explaining his relationship to Grant Sherman's investigation. He also identified the man in the photo. Taking the letter to the Mail Boxes R Us by the Seven Eleven a few blocks from his uncle's apartment, Michael paid to have the letter sent overnight delivery via Fed Ex to the Fugitive Unit of the RCMP in Toronto.

With that task completed, Michael went to the subway station to catch the N&R line up to Manhattan. There was something else that he had to do.

* * * * *

Grant and Jo were somewhere over the Mediterranean Sea, and Jo was still apologizing for taking Grant into a trap.

"You even told me that the story about the Ark of the Covenant sounded like a bunch of crap, but I wouldn't listen. I almost got us killed! If it hadn't have been for that African priest's conscience, we would have been floating in the Indian Ocean."

"But we're not," Grant said. "We need to concentrate on what we're going to do when we get home. You know the Priory will probably be waiting for us to come home."

"Where should we go? Who can we trust?"

"I haven't figured that out yet," Grant said. "Michael will have taken the photo to the authorities by the time we get back to the United States."

"That poor boy is in danger, too!" Jo said.

* * * * *

Michael made his way from the N&R line to the green line, which would take him up to the East Side and the office of the Archdiocese of New York. He stared out the windows of the express subway train at the darkness of the tunnel, which was momentarily broken by the florescent lighting of a local station. The darkness of the tunnel resumed, but Michael's train of thought never wavered. He was deciding what to say to the man responsible for the death of the father he had only recently discovered. He would never get a chance to know the father he had always dreamed of finding.

The train stopped at the next station, and Michael walked out onto the platform with a hundred other people, moving en mass toward the stairs leading to the daylight of Third Avenue. It would be a few blocks of walking to the archdiocese office.

As he entered the waiting area, Michael walked up to the secretary/receptionist and said that he had an appointment to see Archbishop Moreau.

"May I have your name, please?"

"Patrick Murray," Michael said as he selected a copy of *National Catholic Reporter* from the magazine stand and took a seat.

"I'll tell his eminence you're here," the secretary said lifting the receiver form its cradle.

"Thank you."

It was less than a minute later that the secretary informed Michael that the archbishop would see him. Dropping his newspaper on his seat, Michael walked through the door and followed the secretary to the office of Archbishop John Moreau.

"So it's you, Mr. Dennis!" the archbishop said as his curiosity was satisfied. He shook hands with Michael and closed the door behind them. "What can I do for you?"

"I think you've done quite enough already," Michael said sarcastically.

"I'm not sure I know what you mean."

"You killed my father and David Owens and God knows who else."

"You don't know what you are saying."

"Save it, John, or should I say, Patrick?" Michael said handing a copy of the Interpol photograph to the archbishop. Taking the photo, Archbishop John Moreau looked down at himself, although the nose was different and the hair was not as thin as the computer had guessed, the photo was undoubtedly a photo of him. "I know you are Patrick Murray, IRA fugitive and now John Moreau, the leader of the Priory of Sion."

"And who else knows this little bit of information?"

"You don't think I'd be stupid enough to come here before I had made sure the world will know your secret, do you?"

"You still haven't answered my question, Mr. Dennis," the archbishop replied, remaining surprisingly calm.

"I have written to the representatives of Interpol who supplied that photo of you from your IRA days. Grant Sherman gave me the photo, so he knows, too."

"You're very resourceful, Mr. Dennis."

"And you're a murderer!"

"That word is a little strong. People in organizations like the IRA and the Priory of Sion do what has to be done."

"Funny, that's why I'm here – to do what has to be done."

"What do you mean?" the archbishop asked nervously, as Michael produced an air pistol loaded with a wildlife anesthetist's dart.

"You gave a lethal injection to my father. I finally see the idea behind Exodus 21:23 & 24," Michael said walking toward the archbishop, whose eyes widened. The archbishop knew exactly what Michael Dennis had in mind, but to emphasize his point, Michael recited the verses, "…you shall give life for life, eye for eye, tooth for tooth…"

"Now wait a minute – you can't just…"

"Kill you? You don't know me very well, John."

"You won't get away with it – you can't take the law into your own hands. You'll go to jail!"

"That's the beauty of ricin poison. It is easy to obtain and prepare, and twice as toxic as cobra venom. When injected into the bloodstream in this dosage, it causes necrosis of the muscles, especially the heart and lungs. In short, you will have a heart attack and respiratory failure."

"It will leave traces. Poisons always leave traces," the archbishop said with increasing nervousness.

"Not exactly. They might find traces of the anesthetic that's mixed in with the ricin, but ricin is a protein and is rapidly synthesized by the body. The ricin will be gone before you will." Michael said, pulling the trigger of the air pistol. The archbishop instinctively covered his face and tried to turn his back, so the anesthetist's dart struck him under the left arm.

Fear showed in the archbishop's face, as he felt the rapid effects of the tranquilizer. He wanted to run, but couldn't. He wanted to call out, but couldn't. Everything was getting fuzzy, as he fell on his face across the desk.

Michael walked over and removed the dart, and placed it in his pocket. Opening the door a crack, he saw the hall outside the office was empty. Walking quickly but calmly, Michael walked past the secretary into the waiting area.

"Thank you!" he said in a cheerful voice without looking up.

"You're welcome!" the secretary said to his back as he went out the main door. It was the most fun he had ever had in his life.

CHAPTER TWENTY-SIX

The ambulance crew hurried into the office of Archbishop John Moreau, who had been found, slumped over his desk.

"I don't know how long he has been this way," she said as the paramedics began to look for vital signs. "Is he alive?" the secretary asked with great concern.

"Yes, I have a pulse," said one of the paramedics. "Does he have a heart condition?"

"No, I don't think so."

"Is he on any medication?"

"He takes Lipitor© for his cholesterol, but that's all."

"His pupils are fixed and dilated," the second, taller paramedic said. "He's got something in his system. We better transport him ASAP!"

"Can you contact his personal physician, ma'am?" the first paramedic said. It was not a question as much as it was a polite order.

"I guess so."

The archbishop was placed on a gurney and removed to the ambulance outside, where an ambulance-chasing photographer got the shot, which would be on the front page of the next day's *New York Post.*

* * * * *

As Mark O'Shay was about to cross the Delaware River into Pennsylvania, his cell phone chirped. He removed it from his belt and answered as he also dug for two quarters for the toll bridge.

"Yeah?" Mark said into the phone, which he pinched between his head and shoulder, while throwing his change into the catch basket at the tollbooth.

"Mark! It's Grant."

"Where the hell are you?"

"I'm just about to walk aboard a flight here in London for Newark."

"London?" Mark asked showing his confusion. "I thought you went to Africa."

"It's a long story. I'll fill you in later. Can you meet me at Newark Airport?"

"Sure, what flight?"

"British Airways flight 72. We land in about nine hours."

"I'll be there. And Grant…"

"Yes?"

"If I'm a little late, wait for me. Don't leave," Mark said as he pushed the end button.

"Mark? Mark, wait!"

"What happened?" Jo asked Grant.

"He hung up before I could tell him to call the police and have them meet us."

"Call him back," Jo suggested.

"We don't have time, they already made the final boarding call," Grant said. "We can't miss the flight."

"Let's go, you can call him from the plane later."

* * * * *

Michael Dennis followed the ambulance to the hospital. From the parking garage, he called the FBI and told the duty agent that international fugitive Patrick Murray, the IRA bomber, was about to be admitted to Mercy Hospital in Manhattan. Michael told the agent that Interpol and the RCMP had computer-aged photos of Patrick Murray that would prove what he was saying.

After hanging up with the FBI, Michael called the *New York Post* and *The Daily News* and gave them both the story, adding that Patrick Murray had been hiding as a priest in New York City. *This place will be a zoo in about half an hour.* Michael locked his car and walked toward the emergency room, wearing a black suit with the white collar of a Catholic priest.

* * * * *

Mark O'Shay thanked Sister Therese La Sue for the list, assuring her that he would alert the appropriate authorities. Sister Therese said a short prayer for Mark's safety, which made him uncomfortable. Mark had stopped asking God for assistance long ago.

After calling directory assistance for the phone number of the FBI office in New York City, Mark dialed the number and asked to speak to an agent. After about twenty seconds on hold, Mark was connected.

"Special Agent Moore, how can I assist you?"

"I know this might sound unusual…"

"Believe me, sir, I've just about heard it all."

"Yes, I imagine you have. My name is Mark O'Shay, and I work for the Archdiocese of New York."

"Okay," said the agent writing down the name.

"I have convincing evidence that Archbishop John Moreau is in reality an international fugitive wanted in Great Britain for some IRA bombings."

"You won't believe this, but you are the second person that has called today about this. We are already in contact with Interpol. They are sending us a photo of Patrick Murray."

"That's the guy – Patrick Murray. He's still involved in some clandestine activities even now!" Mark said, quite surprised at the ease with which his plan was proceeding.

"We have already sent several agents to the hospital."

"The hospital?" Mark repeated.

Realizing that he had given out unknown information, Agent Moore backpedaled, and changed the subject.

"Could I have your work number and your Social Security Number for identification purposes?" the agent asked. Mark provided the requested information along with his cell phone number to the agent. After writing down the information, the agent thanked Mark for his assistance and hung up the phone.

Mark immediately called his secretary at the archdiocese and asked whether or not Archbishop Moreau was in. As he suspected, the archbishop had been taken to the emergency room at Mercy Hospital. Looking at his watch, Mark figured he could be there in about an hour.

Mark needed to inform the guardians of what he was doing. This was his chance to move up to the leadership council of the Priory. Making another call to Grant Sherman's office number, he waited for the beep and spoke to the guardians that he knew were listening to the line.

"Okay, I have proven my loyalty. I have recovered the list you were worried about and made sure that all other copies have been eliminated. The archbishop's goose is cooked – the FBI and Interpol have discovered his true identity. I can eliminate the threat of his cooperation with authorities, using the same method you used before. I am on my way to the hospital in Manhattan. Grant Sherman and the girl will be flying in to Newark Airport from London later tonight. I will meet them at the airport and clean up all the loose ends."

The guardians, listening to the message, passed word up to their superiors, who were pleasantly surprised with Mark O'Shay, whose loyalty to the Priory had been questioned early on in this crisis. His application for membership to the inner council of the Priory of Sion, which had been rejected before, would be reconsidered should he complete his intended tasks. It would be this inner council that would be electing the new "John" to replace John Moreau.

The Easton, Pennsylvania Fire Department responded to the fire alarm at Notre Dame High School. The fire had started in the computer lab and destroyed one quarter of the building before the sprinkler system and the firemen were able to subdue the blaze. Everyone appeared to have gotten out of the building safely, with the exception of Sister Therese La Sue, who was still missing.

* * * * *

"May I help you, Father?" an emergency room nurse asked Michael Dennis as he strolled among the beds in the back of the ER.

"I hope so," he said smiling. "I was looking for Archbishop John Moreau – he was brought in earlier. Could you direct me?"

"He has been stabilized and moved upstairs for observation," the nurse said. "I'll get you the room number."

"Thank you," Michael said as the nurse walked away. *I bet I really scared that old bastard! I wonder if the Verced© has worn off enough for him to have regained consciousness yet? I should get an Academy Award for my performance. He thought he was really going to die.* Michael was chuckling to himself as the nurse returned.

"He has been moved up to room 317, Father."

"Thank you again."

"You're welcome, Father."

The door to room 317 was open, and Archbishop Moreau was in the bed by the window. Michael walked up to the archbishop's bedside, looking closely at his eyes to make sure that he was still unconscious. With his face less than a foot away from the archbishop's Michael was startled when he heard the voice.

"Is there something I can help you with, pal?"

Michael jumped noticeably and turned to face a tall, blonde man dressed in a blue suit, white shirt, and red tie. The man had obviously entered the room immediately after Michael had.

"You scared me," Michael said.

"Sorry," the man in the suit said. "We would prefer that this patient didn't have any visitors."

"I'm from the archdiocese," Michael lied.

"I figured that when I saw your collar, but still, we are not sure what happened to the archbishop, and..."

"Who is we?" Michael asked.

"I'm Special Agent Jim Wyler, FBI." The agent reached into his jacket pocket and produced a credential with the light blue letters "FBI" printed in one-inch letters on it. The small gold badge on the outside of the black credential case caught the light as the agent whipped the identification open for Michael to read.

"I'm the one who called you about this being Patrick Murray. I knew he was here at the hospital because I followed him here in the ambulance. He was brought here because I knocked him out with a dose of Verced©, so he wouldn't escape. He should wake up any minute now."

"You gave him Verced© to knock him out and called the FBI?"

"That's right. I'm Michael Dennis," he reached out his hand, and the agent shook it. "Patrick Murray here killed my father. Oh, and I'm not really with the archdiocese – I'm only a fourth-year seminarian at Immaculate Conception Seminary on Long Island."

"Do you have any ID with you, Mister Dennis?" the agent asked politely, taking notes on a small, spiral notebook with a black, U.S. Government issued pen.

"Sure, oh, and I did tell the archbishop – or Patrick Murray here that I was shooting him with a deadly poison, but I was just kidding. I wanted him to know what it was like to be on the other side of murder. Maybe it gave him an insight that will help him change his ways."

"I doubt it. Would you be willing to come to the FBI office at 26 Federal Plaza tomorrow and make a full, signed statement?"

"Sure! I'd be glad to. I'm glad that he's in your hands now. What time should I come in?"

"I'm going to be here pretty late, so why don't we make it tomorrow afternoon, say one o'clock?" The agent handed Michael a business card.

"I'll be there Agent Wyler," Michael said, leaving the hospital room. Patrick Murray, alias John Moreau, the leader of the Priory of Sion was in custody, and Michael was happy and proud of the small role he was able to play in bringing his father's killer to justice.

* * * * *

Fire and police investigators recovered what was believed to be the body of Sister Therese La Sue while conducting a joint crime scene search. The burn pattern on the scorched, tile floor indicated that an accelerant like gasoline or paint thinner had been used, making this arson. It was probable that the fire had been set to cover a homicide.

"Call the phone company and pull all her toll calls for the past two weeks," the investigator from the Easton Police Department said to his rookie partner. "Who would have a reason to kill a nun?" he asked, not expecting an answer.

"Should we request an autopsy?" the rookie asked his training partner.

"Of course! Hell, Styles, she was most likely dead before the fire was started. We have to try to find out how she was killed. What kind of stupid question is that?"

* * * * *

Mark O'Shay walked past several news camera crews, which were being refused access to any of the floors that housed patients' rooms. The apparent heart attack of Archbishop John Moreau was a good story for the media vultures. Showing his identification as an employee of the archdiocese and obtaining the archbishop's room number quietly from the reception desk, Mark made his way to the elevator and pressed the number three. A quick thought prompted him to turn off his cell phone to avoid an incoming call at an inopportune moment.

The hallway to the patient rooms on the third floor was unusually quite. In fact, Mark noticed that many of the rooms were completely empty, which would make his job even easier. Dressed in a navy sport coat and khaki Dockers©, Mark stopped at the men's room to relieve himself. It always happened when he was nervous, whether before a big softball game in college or before a big murder.

As he opened the door to return to the hallway, Mark met a man on his way into the men's room. The tall, blonde man was dressed in a blue suit with a white shirt and a red tie. Mark nodded a silent greeting to the man and resumed his search for room 317, which he found rather quickly.

The archbishop was in the bed by the window, asleep. Mark removed the syringe of motor oil from his right hand jacket pocket, and inserted the needle into the part of the I.V. tube especially designed for injections. He was in and out of the room in less than a minute, and the heart monitor alarm went off before Special Agent Wyler had his pants pulled back up.

Archbishop John Moreau died in four minutes after a severe heart attack. The FBI sent agents to Immaculate Conception Seminary to find Michael Dennis. It was too much of a coincidence – the seminarian had said that the archbishop had killed his father. He claimed that he had only knocked the archbishop out, but the seminarian admitted that he had told the archbishop that he was going to kill him.

"Where did he get that much Verced© to knock somebody out for that long?" Agent Wyler's Supervisory Special Agent asked.

"I didn't think to ask him," Agent Wyler replied.

"Didn't think? You're damn right you didn't think! I can't believe you let this guy just walk out of here!"

"I got his identifying information, he's a seminary student for the love of Pete!"

"Call NYPD Homicide and have them get this body to the morgue. We need to know what killed him, so we know how bad it is going to look for us. God damn it!"

* * * * *

"There is motor oil in her heart," the Easton medical examiner repeated, having just completed the autopsy on Sister Therese La Sue.

"Is that what killed her?" the detective asked.

"That would do it alright – cause a complete heart failure. It's a lethal injection."

"I'll get on the VICAP computer and look for any similar homicide cases. It's a new one on me!" The detective said as left the M.E.'s office.

The VICAP computer gave homicide detectives all over the United States a database to search for similar cases, similar victim profiles, similar subject descriptions, but especially similar modus operandi, or M.O.s.

Injecting motor oil into the bloodstream was not a common M.O., so if it had been done before, it would probably be of interest to the Easton Police. After a few minutes of typing, the Easton VICAP operator had located the death of Father Paul Quinn on Long Island by an injection of motor oil while at a hospital.

"Holy shit!" the detective said. "That kid goes to the same seminary where the other motor oil victim taught! I'm going to call the FBI in New York."

* * * * *

The first thing Grant did when their plane landed in Newark Airport was to call his office and listen to his messages. He was quite shocked when he heard Mark O'Shay's message for the guardians, which called Grant and Jo "loose ends." One thing was sure – they would not be going anywhere with Mark O'Shay. Grant filled Jo in on the situation.

"What the hell are we going to do? He probably has a gun, and he'll be waiting for us just outside of customs." she said.

"He won't do anything in public, and we have another advantage. Mark doesn't know that we're on to him. We can slip out to the taxi stand after we clear customs, he'll be waiting for us where the limo drivers and family members wait."

Meanwhile, back in Grant's office, one of the guardians pressed the erase button on the answering machine. They had been listening when Grant accessed his messages. Realizing their mistake, they made sure that there would at least be no more evidence of Mark O'Shay's call for the police to find. Picking up the phone, the guardian dialed Mark O'Shay's cell phone to alert him that Grant was on to him.

"Message W7YY – The cellular telephone subscriber you are calling is not available, or has traveled outside the coverage area. Please try your call again later."

CHAPTER TWENTY-SEVEN

Special Agent Jim Wyler had spoken to the detective from Easton, Pennsylvania, who advised him to call the Suffolk County Police on Long Island. The agent had all the facts on the first two motor oil murders. Now he was hearing the same M.O. once again from the Assistant Medical Examiner of New York City, who had just left the table where he had been watching the autopsy of Archbishop John Moreau.

"I called as soon as we found something," the Assistant M.E. told Special Agent Wyler. "The autopsy's still going on, but we found motor oil inside the heart, so it was obviously murder. The killer probably injected the oil into the patient's I.V. tube."

"Shit! That kid from the seminary, Michael Dennis, is some kind of serial killer."

After hanging up the phone, Special Agent Wyler requested an All Points Bulletin to be sent to all police agencies in the tri-state area, describing Michael Dennis, who was to be considered to be armed and dangerous.

Meanwhile, a U.S. Customs agent was asking Grant and Jo why they were traveling from Africa without any luggage.

"It's kind of a long story," Grant said. "We had to come home suddenly, the hotel is sending our luggage."

"And, why did you have to leave in such a hurry?" the agent didn't like stories that didn't fit the normal pattern of the average international traveler.

"Someone tried to kill us!" Jo said. "Why don't you tell him?" Grant was barely able to contain a groan. "They are a group called the guardians," Jo continued. "One of their members is waiting for us right now in this terminal. Can you give us protection?"

"Could I have your passports please?" the customs agent asked.

"Grant, here, used to be an FBI agent. Call them, they'll tell you!" Jo said.

"Could you follow me to the interview room?" the customs agent asked. Raising his radio to his mouth, he requested the FBI agent on airport duty to meet him at interview room 5.

The walk to the interview room was like the walk to the electric chair for Grant. He knew what was going to happen when the FBI found out that it was he making more wild accusations about mysterious criminals at another airport. *They already think I'm a nut. This is just going to cement that perception in their minds. OH, SHIT!* Grant couldn't believe his eyes. The FBI agent walking to meet them was Special Agent Kirk Wiseman, the same agent who had interviewed him after the LaGuardia Airport kidnapping fiasco.

Special Agent Wiseman recognized Grant immediately, but said nothing. After the customs agent briefed Special Agent Wiseman on the details of the matter, Wiseman thanked the customs agent and politely dismissed him.

"I think I can handle everything from here on," Special Agent Wiseman said, closing the door to the interview room.

"You do airport duty a lot, don't you?" Grant said to try to break the mood.

"Mister Sherman, I warned you once before about this kind of behavior."

"I know; I was just trying to help this lady get home. She had a bad situation in Africa – someone mugged her. She is feeling really vulnerable, so I was just trying to help." Jo looked at him with a confused look, but he met her look with a cold stare. "If you could just have security escort us out to my car, we will be out of your hair – no problems – no reports, please?"

"I'll have security take you to the parking lot if you promise to leave the airport immediately. And if I ever see you again, you'll be spending serious time in jail!" Special Agent Wiseman said with conviction. *What a whack job!*

"You got a deal, Agent Wiseman. Thank you very much," Grant said smiling.

Special Agent Wiseman radioed for a security escort to meet him at interview room 5. After only a few minutes, there was a knock at the door. Opening the door, the FBI agent showed his credentials to the uniformed security officer.

"I need you to escort these people to their vehicle. Where are you parked, Mister Sherman?"

"As close to the terminal as you can get in the daily lot – Area B-5, the first space right by the concrete barrier and the sidewalk to the terminal."

"Sounds easy enough," said the security guard, whose nametag read, "Mata." He was short and overweight, with dark hair. Grant guessed that he was Mexican or perhaps Cuban American.

"Are you originally from Mexico?" Grant asked.

"Don't talk to him!" Special Agent Wiseman said, looking sternly at Grant. "Officer Mata, please take these two directly to their vehicle and make sure they leave!"

"Yes, sir!" Officer Mata said. "You heard the man. Let's go."

As soon as Grant and Jo entered the main terminal from the customs area, Mark O'Shay saw them, as well as the security officer that accompanied them. He would not be able to intercept them quietly. Plan B was now in effect.

Mark walked directly to the Air France ticket counter and purchased a ticket to Paris under the name John Shay, which was the name on his recently acquired passport from Belize. Using a Visa credit card issued to the same name to purchase his ticket, Mark O'Shay ceased to exist.

The walk to Grant's PT Cruiser took only five or six minutes. Officer Mata, who had been leading the way to the parking space Grant had described stopped and stood next to Jo.

"Is this it?" Officer Mata asked, pointing to the purple PT Cruiser in the first space in Area B-5 of the daily lot.

"Yes," Grant said, pulling his keys from his pocket. As the keys came out, several rolled up twenties fell to the concrete of the sidewalk. Grant bent to pick up his money and pressed the button on the remote key ring to unlock the doors, debris from the explosion cut Officer Mata off at the waist. The PT Cruiser was completely obliterated, leaving a small crater in the parking lot. The windows of most of the nearby vehicles were blown out, and car alarms were beeping like crazy. Jo was nowhere to be seen. Grant, who had been partially shielded by the corner of a mini van, was bleeding from the ears. He had been knocked flat on his back and his face had been burned, but he was alive. He got to his feet and staggered away from the site of the explosion, which he knew would soon be crawling with cops. He was dizzy from a concussion and could not hear, but he had to get away so the Priory would think they had accomplished their mission.

At the far end of the daily parking lot by the road, Grant threw up. Still feeling light-headed, he crossed the road and found a drainage culvert in a ditch on the other side. Crawling into the culvert, he found a pipe large enough for a man to crawl through. Once he was far enough up the pipe to feel safe, Grant rolled onto his back and passed out.

When the airport was finally reopened several hours later, John Shay calmly boarded his flight for Paris, where he was planning to attend the seminary to become a Catholic priest. He was quite sure that there were no more loose ends.

By the time the FBI determined that Michael Dennis had also known one of the airport bomb victims, the New York Police Department had already arrested Michael and charged him with first-degree murder for the deaths of Father Paul Quinn, Sister Therese La Sue, and Archbishop John Moreau. He would also become the leading suspect in the bombing deaths of Grant Sherman, Jo Wheeler, and security officer Jose Mata. According to the newspapers, Michael's uncle, Joseph Komkovsky, had hired the best mob attorneys money could buy for his nephew's defense. The basis of that defense would be that a large, secret, underground, religious society was behind the murders of all five victims. The defense intended to show that fear of exposure was the motive for all of the killings, including Archbishop John Moreau, who had actually been the leader of the secret society until his true identity as IRA fugitive Patrick Murray was discovered. The FBI had no comment except that the case was being handled on the local level, with some FBI technical assistance.

In reality, a task force had been formed that included Detective Kevin Brown of the Suffolk County Police, the Easton Police Department detective who had discovered the body of Sister Therese La Sue, a homicide detective from the Midtown Manhattan Precinct of the NYPD, two officers of the New York Port Authority Police – which has authority over crimes at the New York airports, and finally FBI Special Agents Jim Wyler and Kirk Wiseman, who were less than thrilled to be there.

The lead investigator was Detective Kevin Brown from Suffolk County, who was convinced that Michael Dennis had killed his father, the Reverend Father Paul Quinn, because he had abandoned Michael and his family years ago. The murder of seminarian David Owens was also attributed to Michael Dennis, who attempted to make it appear that Owens had done the crime and then committed suicide. The secretary at the Archdiocese of New York identified Michael Dennis from a photo array as the man who had been in Archbishop John Moreau's office just prior to the archbishop being discovered unconscious on his desk. It was also known that Grant Sherman had been hired to investigate the assault on Father Quinn, and during his investigation, Grant Sherman had spoken to Michael Dennis several times. Michael Dennis not only knew four of the victims, but he had recent contact with them. Two of the victims known to Michael Dennis had been killed by injection of motor oil, which made the murder of Sister Therese La Sue in Pennsylvania also attributable to Michael Dennis by circumstantial evidence. Jo Wheeler and Jose Mata were considered unintended victims killed by collateral damage during the murder of Grant Sherman, so all of the deaths could be logically linked to Michael Dennis.

CHAPTER TWENTY-EIGHT

Joseph Komkovsky sat in his apartment feeling overwhelmed. He had three lawyers working on Michael's case. He had just gotten off the phone with the lawyer who was supposed to be getting Michael released on bail when there was a loud knock on the door.

"Who is it?" Joseph yelled, but there was no answer. He walked over and opened the door. "I said who is…" Joseph looked into the face of a man who was supposed to be dead. "You! They said…"

"Yeah, they're saying a lot of things. I know how we can prove Michael is innocent," Grant said, his face had been lacerated in several places by flying glass and the whole right side of his face had blistered. Part of his hair had been burned away on the side of his head, and he had a black eye. In short, he looked like hell.

"Come in, Mister Sherman, come in. Can I get you anything?"

"We might need some of your enforcers," Grant said, "but I'm sure we can get the evidence we need." Grant was still feeling the effects of shock, but he had a purpose. He had to find a way to get the FBI on the right track, save Michael, and avenge Jo's death.

"Everything I have is at your disposal," Joseph Komkovsky said. "Anything you need!"

"First of all, can I crash here for a few days? I want everyone to assume I'm dead for the time being."

"Of course, you're more than welcome. How can we prove that Michael is innocent?" Joseph asked.

"Do you have someone in the Seychelles?" Grant asked.

"Of course!"

"I don't care how you do it, but there is a short, thin, African priest in the only Catholic church in Victoria town center on the Island of Mahe'. We need him here in the states as a witness. If you sneak him in without a visa, we'll have more leverage on him."

"What else do you need?"

"I need the computer from a gallery in Salem, Massachusetts called The Simple Things. The owner of that gallery died in the explosion at the airport. There is a list of all priests who are members of The Priory of Sion saved in the memory of that computer."

"I have friends in Boston. Let me make a few calls."

"Do you mind if I take a shower?"

"My house is your house, Mister Sherman. I'll have someone from the clothing store bring you several new things to wear."

Grant thanked him and went into the bathroom. His reflection in the mirror was a shock. His face didn't hurt as much as one would assume by looking at it. Before he began running the water in the shower, Grant heard Joseph Komkovsky talking on the phone with some of his "friends." *Those bastards are going to be sorry they screwed with the Russian Mafia and me!*

With the water as cold as he could stand it, Grant let it pour over his head, carefully rubbing his fingers over his face in an attempt to remove the dried blood. In one of the deeper cuts, he found a small cube of glass imbedded. With a great deal of pain, he was able to remove it.

After toweling off his body, Grant dried his tender face and applied some first aid cream that he found in the medicine chest. Although the first aid cream appeared to be left over from the Carter administration, Grant figured it was better than nothing. He applied a Band-Aid© to the cut from which he had removed the glass and combed what was left of his hair back with his fingers. *At least I don't look like Frankenstein's monster anymore!*

Grant wore Joseph's robe out into the apartment, where his host was on another telephone call.

"How many Catholic churches can there be in Victoria town center? It's tiny!"

"Tell him it's a block from the clock," Grant suggested.

"One block from the clock," Joseph repeated. "Why didn't I say so? Listen you – You owe me, and this will square us. Don't screw this up." Joseph hung up the phone and turned to his guest. "So, you look much better!"

"Thanks."

"Your clothes are on the way. I got your size from those old things," Joseph motioned to the dirty pile of what was left of Grant's clothes.

"I take it the priest from Africa will be coming to visit the US?"

"And the computer will be here by tomorrow morning," Joseph said with a smile. "You should have left the FBI sooner and come to work for me. We get things done!"

"Right now, I don't want to think about the FBI. They and the police have this case so screwed up! How could they think Michael killed all those people?"

"They think that because he is my nephew, Mister Sherman."

"Please, call me Grant."

"And you can call me Joseph."

"The FBI always thinks the worst of people like me. They always treat us with suspicion and assume the worst. If they only would try to understand our way of life and show us some respect, we could exist together. I don't do any serious crimes, and I have never seriously hurt anyone."

Grant was amused by the adverb and wondered how much pain constituted being seriously hurt.

"Well, we're allies now, Joseph."

"Yes, allies. Would you like to rest now? I can show you to your bedroom."

"That would be great," Grant said with a yawn.

"By the time you wake up, the computer will be here."

* * * * *

Grant awoke at seven in the morning to find several new changes of clothes folded on the floor at the foot of the bed. He dressed in a polo shirt and khaki slacks. There were even two pair of shoes, from which Grant chose the brown topsiders. He decided to forgo the agony of shaving although Joseph had left a razor and shaving cream on the floor with the clothes and shoes. There was also a new toothbrush, comb, and a tube of Close Up© toothpaste, for which Grant was most grateful.

Walking down the hall to the kitchen, Grant saw Joseph watching the morning news on television as Michael's mother, Nellie Dennis, prepared breakfast.

"Good Morning, Grant" Joseph said. "You have met my niece, Nellie."

"Of course. How are you?" Grant asked.

"Much better since Uncle Joseph has told me about your help."

"I can only do what's right. Michael is a good boy."

"Thank you, Mister Sherman."

"Call me Grant."

"Okay," she smiled, "Grant."

"The computer came early this morning," Joseph said. "It is all set up on the dining room table."

Grant went to the dining room and sat down at the computer and turned it on. Joseph's "friends" had brought the tower, monitor, keyboard, printer, mouse, even the mouse pad from Jo's computer. Grant opened Outlook and found Jo's stored e-mails, for which no password was needed. However, the attachment to the coded e-mail message from Father Quinn was password protected. The receiver of a password protected attachment gets a notice that a password is required to open the attachment.

"I don't have my programs with me," Grant said. "Do you know a hacker with a password breaking program?"

"Nyetu problemu," Joseph said in Russian. He walked over to the phone and made a call.

In less than half an hour, a young, Russian man was at the front door. He was about 24 or 25 and wore black jeans and black shoes with a sport shirt that buttoned down the front. His long brown hair was not clean, but it had been combed.

"Vam nuzhen computerni expert?" The Russian asked.

"Da, nuzhen. Program y vac est dla password?" Joseph asked in Russian.

"Est. Nyetu problemu."

"He has the program," Joseph said. "I told you – nyetu problemu."

The young Russian sat down and at the computer. Grant had already highlighted the e-mail attachment that needed the password. The Russian tried to open the attachment and received the prompt asking for a password. Inserting a CD into the disc drive, he began the same random sequence program that Sister Therese La Sue had used to crack the password protect feature on Father Quinn's computer before.

"I can take it from here, Joseph," Grant said. Joseph peeled a few hundreds off a roll of cash in his pocket and handed them to the young Russian, who smiled and left quietly.

"How long will it take?" Nellie asked.

"Probably five or six hours if we're lucky," Grant said.

* * * * *

Seven and a half hours after the program was begun, the password appeared on the prompt line, and the list of priests who were members of the Priory of Sion filled the monitor screen.

"We got it!" Grant said from behind a McDonald's© bag. "By God, we've got them now!"

"Print it! Print it!" Nellie said. Her excitement came from the promise of saving her beloved Michael from jail.

"Now it's up to your friends, Joseph. Somehow we have to find some of the priests on this list and make them talk to us."

"Grant, I have friends who have very interesting ways to make people talk," Joseph said with a smile.

"That's one of the reasons I came to you in the first place. We'll fight fire with fire. First, we have to figure out a way to determine which of these names are assigned in the New York area," Grant said.

"Michael's friend from the seminary has asked how he can help," Nellie said. "He might be able to get some kind of directory from the seminary."

"Get him here!" Grant said. "What's his name?"

"His name is Greg. He and Michael were roommates."

It took Greg less than an hour to get to Joseph's apartment, where he went over the list that Grant had printed from Jo's computer. Having stolen a directory of all the priests in the Archdiocese of New York from the seminary's office, it was simply a matter of comparing Father Quinn's list to the names in the directory.

Grant and Greg worked quickly and silently for twenty minutes before they found a match.

"Here's one!" Greg said, pushing his smeared glasses back up on his face. "Father Peter Case at Saint Jude's in Queens." Grant wrote the name and address on a yellow pad of paper.

It took them over an hour to search for the seventy-four names from Father Quinn's list of Priory members in the directory of priests from the Archdiocese of New York. In the end, Grant and Greg located seven in New York City and another five in northern New Jersey. Grant handed the list to Joseph.

"We will need to 'interview' some of these priests, Joseph," Grant said with a wink.

"I have just the men for the job, do you want to go along?"

"I think I could just send a list of questions," Grant said. "That way you could send several teams and cover more ground."

"I think that's a good idea," Joseph said.

The first of three pairs of muscle-bound mercenaries called on Father Peter Case at St. Jude's Catholic Church in the Richmond Hills area of Queens. It was a rough, blue-collar neighborhood that had mostly Puerto Rican and Irish American residents. Knocking on the front door of the rectory, Joseph's friends asked to speak to Father Pete.

"Do you have an appointment?" the lady at the door asked. She thought it was her duty to protect the priests from their over-demanding parishioners.

"My father is dying," the smaller of the Russian thugs said with believable feeling. "He asked me to bring Father Pete to give him the last rites. He thinks Father Pete is the best priest here."

"Oh, well, I'll tell him you're here."

The lady returned quickly with a man who was obviously Father Peter Case.

"What is the address we're going to?" the priest asked.

"400 Hillsdale Avenue," the taller thug answered without a hitch.

"Okay, should I follow you?" Father Case asked.

"That's okay, or you can just ride with us. The address is not easy to find."

"I can ride with Father Pete," the taller thug suggested. "That way he won't get lost."

"Fine, let's go," the priest said, looping the strap of his kit of holy water and other essentials over his head.

After driving several blocks, the lead car pulled over to the curb.

"Why are we stopping here?" Father Case asked.

"We're leaving your car here," the taller Russian said, aiming a semi-automatic 9mm pistol at the priest's head.

"What do you want from me? I don't carry any money."

"Cool it, Father. Just get in the other car quietly, and I won't have to shoot you."

"Can you tell me what this is about?" Father Case pleaded.

"John Moreau," the Russian said, reading the name from the list of Grant's questions that Joseph had passed on to him.

"I see," said the priest, who exited his vehicle and walked up to the lead car.

"You sit in the front," the taller thug said to the priest, "so I can keep an eye on you."

"Where are you taking me?" the priest asked.

"Someplace where we can talk."

* * * * *

Being a Monday, the Czarina Restaurant was closed as usual. The two Russians, one in front of Father Case and one behind, walked to the rear entrance of the restaurant. Once his eyes adjusted to the darkness, Father Case was surprised to see two of his fellow members of the Priory of Sion, each accompanied by two Russian escorts.

"What is this all about?" Father Case asked again. He received a half-strength blow on the head with the handle of the 9mm pistol for his trouble. The priest was knocked forward and sprawled noisily to the floor.

"We will ask the questions," the taller Russian said. "My name is Misha. We decided to get the three of you together to tell us about the Priory of Sion and the late Archbishop John Moreau, who ran it."

An FBI agent listening to a court ordered, microphone surveillance turned up the volume and placed his hands over his headphones to limit outside noise.

"Call Jim Wyler, I think he's going to want to know about this!" The agent listened as the priests at first denied any knowledge of an organization called the Priory of Sion, but a few jolts from an electric cattle prod changed their attitude.

"If you want to keep lying to us, I can have Slava boil some water. However, I don't believe you will like what he will do with it."

"Okay, okay! We are members of the Priory. For God's sake have mercy!"

"My mercy is directly proportional to the amount of information I receive," Misha said smiling. "Was Archbishop John Moreau the leader of the Priory of Sion?" Misha read the first of Grant's questions from the yellow sheet of paper.

"Yes," Father Case said.

"Do you others agree with that?"

"Yes," the other two priests said at once."

"And do you know that John Moreau ordered the death of Father Paul Quinn?"

There was silence. "Slava, bring the boiling water!"

"It is not hot enough yet," Slava called from the kitchen."

"We're going to have to go in and stop this!" the FBI agent listening to the hidden microphone said to his co-workers, as he pulled the plug of his headphones out of the jack to allow everyone in the room to hear the conversation. The tape recorders were rolling, and now four agents were listening live.

"Call the ASAC!" one of the agents said. "He will have to authorize us to move in on this."

The Russian nicknamed Slava came into the back room of the restaurant with a steaming pan of water. Setting it on the table next to Father Case, he began to tie the priest to the chair.

"We can't have you jumping all over the place when we stick your hand into the pot," he said to Father Case."

"Dear God!"

"God has nothing to do with this, Father Case," Misha said. "Answer the question."

"Yes, Father Quinn was trying to identify all of the priests who were members of the Priory, so he was eliminated, but we didn't have anything to do with that!"

"Did the Priory attack the private investigator, Grant Sherman and his traveling companion in the Seychelles?" Misha read the next question from the list.

Again there was silence, so Slava took a spoon of the steaming water and dribbled it on Father Case's hand. His screams raised goose bumps on the necks of the listening FBI agents.

"Did you get the ASAC yet?" the first agent yelled to the next room.

"They are trying his cell phone, and they beeped him!" came the response.

"Try the SAC, too!"

Back in the back room of the Czarina, Father Case's tongue had loosened quite a bit.

"Yes, they were intercepted in the Seychelles, but they escaped."

"So the Priory sent someone to meet them at the airport, right?" Misha asked.

"Yes."

"You can't tell them this, one of the other two priests said. They'll kill us for revealing this information."

Slava threw a spoonful of scalding water on the priest who had spoken and touched the electric cattle prod to his neck. The screams made the agents squirm in their seats.

"If we don't go in there now, we're going to have hell to pay! Radio the surveillance teams to put on their bulletproof vests and prepare to enter the restaurant."

"Please stop! No more, Father Case said. Everything you said is true. Archbishop Moreau brought in a hit team from France, and they killed Father Quinn and the seminarian at Immaculate Conception. Mark O'Shay killed the Archbishop, because his true identity was known to the police."

"What was his true identity?" Misha asked.

"You know! What are you making me say it? He was Patrick Mur…" Suddenly Father Case froze. He realized why the Russian calling himself Misha wanted him to say everything. This place was bugged, and the Russians knew it! "You bastard!" Father Case said. "You set us up for the FBI!"

"Release them," Slava said. "Our work is finished."

* * * * *

By the time the FBI was prepared to enter the Czarina Restaurant, the three priests were running from the back door of the Czarina and across the parking lot to the street corner. As they tried to hail a cab, an FBI agent pulled his car up to the curb and identified himself to them.

"Could you come with me, please?" the agent asked politely.

"No, we're okay," Father Case said, trying to smile. "We were just going to hail a cab."

"No, you don't understand," the agent said less politely. "Get in the car, all three of you! Now!" A second FBI car pulled up behind the first.

"What about those Russians inside the restaurant?" Father Case asked. "They would have killed us!"

"We'll deal with them later," the agent said. "I think we have some questions about your friends before we worry about your enemies. You can start by telling us where Mark O'Shay is. Then we'll talk about this list that everyone was so interested in getting."

On Tuesday afternoon, Michael Dennis walked out of jail and was greeted by his Great Uncle Joseph, his mother, and Grant Sherman. Uncle Joseph and Grant were smiling, and Michael's mother was crying.

"We'll sue them for false arrest!" Uncle Joseph said loudly with his finger raised.

"Jesus asked God to forgive his persecutors, saying they didn't know what they were doing," Michael said.

"You don't know how true that statement is, Michael," Grant said as he put his arm around Nellie. "Believe me, they didn't have a clue!"

CHAPTER TWENTY-NINE

The list of Catholic priests that were members of the Priory of Sion was published on the front page of the *New York Times* along with the mug shot of Patrick Murray and a recent photo of Archbishop John Moreau. The headline was in one-inch letters: "Murdered Archbishop Was International Fugitive." The story went on to explain that Archbishop John Moreau, who was really IRA bomber Patrick Murray, had been murdered by his own secret cult to protect themselves from exposure when Interpol discovered the true identity of the archbishop. The FBI had no comment other than to say that the investigation was a coordinated effort between the FBI, Interpol, the Royal Canadian Mounted Police, the New York Police Department, the New York Port Authority, and the police departments of several local jurisdictions, including Suffolk County, New York and Easton, Pennsylvania. Since the investigation was still ongoing, the FBI spokesperson refused to release any details other than the fact that at least fifteen suspected members of a secret criminal organization were already in custody, and more arrests were expected soon.

At the office of the FBI at 26 Federal Plaza, a short, thin African priest was handing over a stack of documents, which outlined a complex organization of foreign bank accounts and international corporations, which were really controlled by the Priory of Sion. “If the FBI is able to seize twenty million dollars,” the small priest said, “is it possible for some of the money to go to feed the children of my home village?”

“We’ll have to discuss it with the Assistant United States Attorney,” Special Agent Wyman said, “but I’m sure we can work something out for you. That is done all the time.” He was confident that the priest would be rewarded for his testimony. The agent was also confident that he would be promoted to a Supervisory Special Agent’s position as soon as this case was concluded.

ABOUT THE AUTHOR

Joel Bartow served as a Special Agent for the FBI for ten years from 1987 to 1997. During that time, Bartow was a member of the Russian Organized Crime squad in New York City, conducting complex money laundering investigations with direct assistance from the Russian Ministry of Internal Affairs (MVD). After leaving the FBI, Bartow lived and worked in the Former Soviet Union for one year.

Bartow holds a Master of Arts Degree in Social Science and has written articles on money laundering for *The White Paper,* published by the Association of Certified Fraud Examiners, and for *The Police Chief* the journal of the International Association of Chiefs of Police. Bartow has taught for the Association of Certified Fraud Examiners' Annual Fraud Conferences since 1999.

Bartow is the Managing Partner for Investigations at The Worldwide Investigative Network, LLC in West Chester, Pennsylvania, investigating cases in Russia, Estonia, Ukraine, Antigua, Switzerland, Greece, Israel, Kenya, Nigeria, and all across the United States.

Bartow is also the author of *Looking the Pale Horse in the Mouth. He* lives in Reading, Pennsylvania with his wife and three children.

Printed in the United States
750900004BA